D0273350

SPECIAL MESSAGE TO READERS

THE ULVERSCROFT FOUNDATION
(registered UK charity number 264873)

was established in 1972 to provide funds for
research, diagnosis and treatment of eye diseases.
Examples of major projects funded by
the Ulverscroft Foundation are:-

- The Children's Eye Unit at Moorfields Eye
  Hospital, London
- The Ulverscroft Children's Eye Unit at Great
  Ormond Street Hospital for Sick Children
- Funding research into eye diseases and
  treatment at the Department of Ophthalmology,
  University of Leicester
- The Ulverscroft Vision Research Group,
  Institute of Child Health
- Twin operating theatres at the Western
  Ophthalmic Hospital, London
- The Chair of Ophthalmology at the Royal
  Australian College of Ophthalmologists

You can help further the work of the Foundation
by making a donation or leaving a legacy.
Every contribution is gratefully received. If you
would like to help support the Foundation or
require further information, please contact:

THE ULVERSCROFT FOUNDATION
The Green, Bradgate Road, Anstey
Leicester LE7 7FU, England
Tel: (0116) 236 4325

website: www.foundation.ulverscroft.com

THE GREEN PEN MYSTERY & OTHER STORIES

Caught in a thunderstorm one hot summer night, Peter Lake takes shelter in a public call-box. When the telephone begins to ring, and curiosity prompts him to answer, a desperate plea for help issues from the receiver — then a scream — then silence. His determination to assist the owner of the mystery voice will fling him headlong into uncharted seas of crime, danger and sudden death ... Meanwhile, Adam Kane, brilliant and unorthodox solicitor, brings his powerful intellect to bear on four baffling cases.

DONALD STUART

THE GREEN PEN MYSTERY

& OTHER STORIES

Complete and Unabridged

LINFORD
Leicester

First published in Great Britain

First Linford Edition
published 2016

Copyright © 1934, 1972, 1973 by Gerald Verner
Copyright © 2015 by Chris Verner
All rights reserved

A catalogue record for this book is available
from the British Library.

ISBN 978–1–4448–2737–8

EAST SUSSEX COUNTY LIBRARY	
04165814	
ULV	14 JAN 2016
LEW 11/16	£8.99
LEW 1/19	

Contents

The Green Pen Mystery

1

Wrong Number!

The most trivial decisions have a habit of leading to momentous events. If Peter Lake had not elected to walk home from George Arlington's on that hot summer night, the whole course of his life might have been changed. He would in all probability never have met Lola Marsh, remained ignorant of the existence of the elusive 'Mr. K.', and avoided the danger and unpleasantness surrounding the green fountain pen belonging to the unfortunate Harvey Slade.

But fate, which is another name for circumstance, willed it otherwise, and so, when he set off along the cool and deserted country lane which led to the village, he took the first step that was to lead him out of the commonplace routine of his daily life and plunge him into an uncharted sea of mystery, danger and sudden death!

He refused George Arlington's offer of a lift because he was a little worried, and hoped that the mile and a quarter walk would produce something in the nature of a solution to the problem that was bothering him. It was a very prosaic problem and centred round a collection of unpaid bills that almost filled a small drawer of the desk in his shabby consulting room, but it was also a very vital problem, and had caused Peter to lose a considerable amount of sleep during the past few weeks.

He needed money urgently — at least three of his creditors were getting unpleasantly pressing — and Peter had not the remotest idea where the money could be obtained. He had sunk every penny of his small capital in the purchase of old Dr. Heppel's practice, and had bitterly regretted it before he had been in occupation a month.

The chief source of income had been an eccentric old lady, who had nothing the matter with her at all except old age, but who liked to have a doctor in daily attendance on her, and was willing to pay for this privilege. Her only complaint had carried her off a fortnight after Peter had moved into the little house on the fringe of the village, and the remainder of his patients were disgustingly healthy.

He had carried on, hoping for the best, and getting more and more into debt until now the crisis was almost at hand. Between now and Saturday — three days — it was absolutely essential that he should find a hundred and fifty pounds, and he hadn't the least idea where to find even a hundred and fifty pence. Nothing short of a miracle or an epidemic could save him from the resultant proceedings.

He lit a cigarette, thrust his hands into the pockets of his dinner-jacket, and frowned.

His last forlorn effort had failed.

It had taken a certain amount of moral courage to ask George Arlington for help, and although George had been very sympathetic, he had made it quite clear that he could do nothing, and sympathy wasn't going to stop Macklinbergs from issuing a writ. The prospect looked black — almost as black as the clouded sky. The association of ideas made him look up, and as he did so a jagged ribbon of blue flickered in the south. It was followed a few seconds later by the low mutter of thunder.

Peter turned up the collar of his jacket and broke into a run, but before he had gone a hundred yards the rain was coming down in torrents. There was no shelter. The lane was narrow, and ran between straggling hedge, enclosed by barbed wire, beyond which lay ploughed fields. He had reached a point where a secondary road bisected the lane, and had resigned himself to a soaking, when in the brilliant glare of the lightning he saw the very thing he wanted.

At the junction of the roads stood a public call-box. Peter made for it as fast as he could, jerked open the door, and stumbled into the interior with a sigh of thankfulness. The rain was falling with almost tropical violence, hissing and splashing round his tiny shelter; the lightning and thunder were almost incessant. However, it was dry enough inside the telephone box, and he could stay until the storm

6

passed over. He took his handkerchief from his pocket, and wiped the wet from his hair and neck, wondering why he had not remembered this place before. He had passed it often enough.

Replacing the handkerchief, he took out a cigarette, and was in the act of feeling for his lighter when the bell behind him rang shrilly — a deafening racket in that confined space. Peter jumped violently and swung round, staring at the dimly seen instrument.

Who the deuce could be ringing up a public call-box? The bell ceased for a moment and then started again — an insistent and prolonged br-r-r —

More from curiosity than anything else, Peter lifted the receiver from its hook and put it to his ear.

'Hello!' he called, and almost instantly there came over the wire the faint, breathless, agitated voice of a girl.

'Jim! Jim! Is that you?' she said, and then before he could answer: 'For heaven's sake come to Slade's at once!'

'I'm afraid — ' began Peter, but the caller went on quickly without listening.

'I'm frightened — horribly frightened.' The tone was frantic; the words jerky and disjointed; barely audible. 'He's locked me in . . . there's something dreadful going on . . . Mr. K. — ' There was a rasping, scraping sound, the echo of a scream, and — silence.

For a second Peter stood still, the memory of that soft frightened voice ringing in his ears, and then he dropped the receiver back on its hook. There was no mistaking the meaning of that scraping sound — someone had cut the telephone wires while the girl had been speaking.

Peter frowned. She had mentioned Slade's. That must mean Harvey Slade, surely — the occupier of the big, gaunt house on the left of the secondary road barely a hundred and fifty yards away. What was going on there? Something pretty bad, apparently. Peter could still hear that terror-laden voice with its urgent appeal. Well, rain or no rain, he wasn't going to leave a girl in that state without seeing what was happening.

He had evidently received a message intended for Jim, whoever he was

— probably the exchange had plugged into the wrong number. He pulled open the door of the little kiosk and stepped out into the downpour. If anything, it had increased, and before he had gone a dozen yards he was soaked to the skin, with his hair hanging in straggling wisps over his forehead.

Locked her in, had they? His thoughts were grim as he splashed his way along the right hand branch of the secondary road. Well, they'd damn well soon have to let her out again. Just the sort of thing he would expect from a man like old Slade — a thin, bald-headed old vulture, hated by everybody in the village and Peter in particular. He was in sight of the house now — a low, rambling building set well back among a cluster of trees — a dark, repellent place with no light visible at any of the windows. A long drive ran up from the road, bordered on either side by high, dense hedges, each leaf a miniature cataract.

Peter entered the open gateway, and as he did so there came from somewhere ahead a muffled cry: a scream of sheer terror that pulled him up in his tracks and stirred the hair on his neck. There was death in that awful cry. It came again, but this time was drowned in the crash of thunder that split the heavens and shook the ground under his feet.

He took a step forward, and then, as the echoes of the thunderclap rumbled to silence, he heard another sound — the sound of someone running rapidly, desperately. He crouched back against the gatepost, his nerves tense, watching the dark tunnel of the drive down which those flying steps were coming. They drew nearer and nearer, and now he could hear the panting breaths of the runner. And then the lightning glared fitfully, and in its bluish radiance he saw the figure of a big man coming towards him with surprising speed considering his bulk.

He straightened up as the man bore down upon him, and shouted to him to stop. The reply he received was unexpected. He heard a muttered oath, then out of the darkness came a stab of flame, and the crack of an automatic. The bullet sped past Peter without danger, but he felt the wind of it unpleasantly close to his right ear.

Peter was not unreasonably annoyed, and as the shooter drew level with him he stepped forward and lashed out with his right. He brought all the weight of his thirteen stone to bear on that blow, and it caught the runner on the side of the jaw. With a yelp of pain, he staggered and fell sprawling. Had it reached the point, as Peter intended it should, he would have stayed down, but as it was it only stunned him for a second, and as Peter stooped over him he kicked out viciously with his feet. One of his heavy boots landed with a terrific impact on Peter's right knee, and he collapsed.

In a second the other was up, and, taking to his heels, disappeared through the gateway into the darkness and rain. Peter scrambled to his feet shakily and painfully. He was smothered in mud from head to foot, and his knee was hurting like the deuce. He tested his weight gingerly on his injured leg, and found that it was not as bad as he thought. He was moving forward, when he trod on something that was hard and round. He thought that it was a stone at first, then the lightning came again and, looking down, he saw something that glinted greenly on the gravel of the path.

Stooping, he picked it up and, striking a match, saw that it was a fountain pen. The big man must have dropped it when he fell. Almost unconsciously, Peter slipped it into his jacket pocket — and from that moment went in danger of his life, for the green fountain pen carried in its train the shadow of death!

2

Mr. K.

Peter made his way slowly up the drive, keeping a wary lookout for anyone else who might be lurking about. But he saw no one. The place was apparently deserted.

Presently he came underneath the dark bulk of the house, and looked up. There was still no light to be seen anywhere, nor could he hear any sound save the swish of the falling rain on the leaves. He went up the steps to the front door and found — rather to his surprise — that it was half-open, the hall beyond in pitch-darkness.

After a momentary hesitation he cautiously crossed the threshold and listened. But still no sound came to his straining ears. An unearthly hush seemed to brood like a living presence over the whole house.

He stood rather undecidedly just inside the doorway. There must be somebody about. From whom had come those horrible screams? And where was the girl whose voice he had heard over the telephone? It was certainly not she who had screamed; the tone had been deeper, that of a man. Of course, she had said something about being locked in.

He hesitated no longer and, moving forward into the darkness of the hall, fumbled along the wall in the hope of finding the electric light switches. After a moment or two he found them and pressing them down, flooded the place with a blaze of light.

The hall was beautifully furnished. The light streaming down from silk-shaded pendants was reflected in the polished furniture and showed up the warm colours of the rugs with which the parquet floor was strewn. Peter, who knew about such things, took a mental note of the pictures on the walls. A Marillo, one or two of Zhon's etchings, a Millais. Old Harvey Slade, for all his reputed meanness, evidently liked to surround himself with good things.

With the lights on, Peter felt a little less uncomfortable. He was still a trifle apprehensive in this silent house; the atmosphere was oppressive, but the light gave the added assurance of sight. He was no longer groping in the dark against a horror that was invisible. Whatever might be lurking in wait for him there, it was a pleasant relief to know that he could see it coming.

Several rooms opened off the hall, but before approaching any of them, he called loudly:

'Anybody at home?'

His voice came back to him with a booming echo from the darkness of the big staircase, but nobody answered. He went over to the first door, pushed it open, switched on the lights, and peered in. It was the dining-room, evidently, and empty. Someone, however, had used it recently, for the centre table was still laid with the remains of a meal.

His frown deepened as he went to the second door. What the deuce was the matter with this house? There was something frightening about this unbroken silence. Surely there were servants in a big place like this — where were they? Mechanically, he glanced at his wristwatch. It was nearly half-past eleven. They couldn't still be out at this hour. And those screams —

He gave an involuntary shudder as he pushed open the second door and looked in. The lights here were on — he had not seen them before because the window gave onto the back of the house — and one glance told him that he need look no farther for an explanation of those terrible cries! It was here, in this lighted room, lying sprawled by the side of the big desk. A twisted figure, whose thin-lipped mouth was contorted into a grin of fear and terror, and from under whose body spread a sinister stain that had soaked into the light carpet.

Peter stared at that dead thing with shrinking eyes. It was old Harvey Slade — there was no doubt of that. The thin face and shining bald head were unmistakable, and the manner of his death had been shocking. A feeling of sick revulsion came over him as he saw the handle of the knife that still protruded from the dead man's throat, and for a second the room swam dizzily. He turned and leaned against the doorpost breathing quickly;

closing his eyes for a moment to shut out that horrible sight. And then, as he opened them again, suddenly and without warning all the lights went out!

Peter felt his breath leave his lungs in a gasp at the sudden shock. In a momentary panic he swung round, groping blindly for the door. It was bad enough in that room with the lights on, but in the dark . . . He almost ran into the hall, but the light there had gone out, too, and he paused irresolutely. And then close behind him he heard the sound of soft breathing. Someone was there in the darkness — almost within arm's length of him. He put out his hands, and they touched rough cloth, and then flesh. He heard a low exclamation — a sharp hiss of indrawn breath — and then something crashed down on his head, and the surrounding blackness rushed into his brain and engulfed his senses . . .

The man who had struck him replaced the spanner in his pocket and flashed the white ray of a torch on the motionless body of his victim. Stooping, he turned Peter over, and gave a little grunt of surprise as he saw his face.

'Now, who the deuce are you?' he muttered, and then: 'All right, Lola, the coast is clear.'

From the direction of the staircase came the faintest sound of a suppressed sob. A soft, light footstep advanced over the thick carpet, and into the circle of light thrown by the torch in the man's hand, came a girl — a dim figure, slim and graceful, with a white face and terror-laden eyes.

'You haven't — you haven't — ' She evidently feared to complete the sentence, but her wide, troubled eyes looked at her companion questioningly.

He shook his head.

'I've only put him to sleep for a few minutes,' he whispered. 'Come on — let's get away from here as quickly as we can.'

'Who is it?' She moved nearer, peering down at Peter's motionless form.

'I haven't the least idea,' said the man with the torch. 'Haven't you seen him before?'

'No.' She laid her hand on his arm, and one of her gloves which she had been carrying fell unnoticed to the floor. 'He — he isn't a — a detective, is he?'

'I shouldn't think so,' replied the other impatiently. 'He doesn't look like one. I only caught a glimpse of him from the top of the staircase when he came in, and while he was in the study I crept down and pulled out the fuses. For heaven's sake, don't let us waste any more time. Come along!'

He took her by the arm and led her over to the front door. On the threshold the girl hesitated and looked back. Her eyes rested for a moment fearfully on the entrance to the room in which the dead thing which had once been a man lay grinning up at the ceiling. And then, at an impatient word from her companion, she turned and followed him into the night.

A minute passed — two — and then from the shadows of the hall came a crouching shape. It tip-toed forward, glancing uneasily over its stooping shoulders. Reaching the side of Peter Lake, it bent down and fumbled about his unconscious body . . .

*　*　*

Alone in the darkness and the silence, Peter stirred uneasily and opened his eyes. His head ached dully, and the blackness around him seemed to be pressing in on all sides — a palpable and material weight.

Memory came back with a sudden rush and he sat up with difficulty, groaning and rubbing his head. He was in the act of scrambling to his feet when he heard the sound of wheels on gravel and the rhythmic throbbing of an engine. A car was coming up the drive, and even as he staggered unsteadily towards the door, it stopped with a squeal of brakes, and there came the muttering of voices.

'Great Scott,' thought Peter in dismay, 'are there any more of them in this business?'

There were, apparently; four more, anyway, for the open doorway suddenly became blocked with men — big men, two of whom held in their hands electric torches. The foremost uttered a sharp exclamation as his light fell upon the swaying, dishevelled figure of Peter, and he advanced and grabbed him by his arm.

'Anything happened 'ere?' he growled in a hard voice.

Peter had an insane desire to laugh.

'Anything happened?' he echoed shakily, and saw for the first time that two of the newcomers were in uniform. 'I'm damn sure that very little more could happen.'

At the sound of his voice a police constable came forward and peered at him closely.

'Why, if it ain't Dr. Lake!' he cried in surprise. 'I thought I knew yer voice, sir. What are you doing here?'

'You know this man, Verney?' snapped the authoritative voice of the man who was gripping Peter's arm.

'Yes, sir,' replied Verney. 'It's Dr. Lake from the village.'

'Humph!' said the hard voice, and Peter felt the fingers that gripped him relax a little. 'Well, perhaps Dr. Lake from the village will explain what he's doing here covered in mud and with all the lights out.' Peter hesitated, and the other went on:

'I'm Detective-Inspector Bullot from Scotland Yard.'

For a moment Peter had a wild idea that the whole thing was a nightmare.

'From Scotland Yard?' he repeated in amazement. 'Then what the deuce are you doing here? How did you know that anything had happened?'

'I'll hear your story first, if you don't mind,' broke in the inspector. 'I can tell you mine later, if necessary.'

Peter pulled himself together, and proceeded to give a brief account of all that occurred since he had sought shelter in the telephone-box, and had the satisfaction of an attentive audience. Only once was he interrupted, and this was when the Yard man barked an order to one of the policemen.

'See if you can do anything about these lights,' he said. 'We can't go groping about in the dark. Sorry. Go on, Doctor!'

Peter finished his story and, as he concluded, the lights came on with a flicker.

'That's better,' grunted the inspector, a heavy-jowled man with a grey wisp of a moustache. 'What was wrong, Verney?'

'Main fuses pulled, that's all, sir,'

reported the constable from the back of the staircase.

Inspector Bullot grunted again.

'Did you see or hear anything of the girl?' he asked, and Peter shook his head.

'I didn't have time to see or hear very much,' he replied. 'What I did see was quite enough to be going on with.'

'You mean the dead man?' The inspector rubbed his chin. 'We had better go and have a look at him. Which room did you say it was — the second one?'

Peter pointed to the half-open door, and the inspector went over to it. Before crossing the threshold he looked back. 'Archer, take Verney and make a thorough search of the house. See if you can find any traces of the woman Dr. Lake mentioned. You, Jackson,' he nodded to the third man who was still standing by the open front door, 'remain on guard here in the hall.'

While he was speaking, Peter happened to glance down at the floor, and it was at this moment that he saw the glove that the girl had dropped. Stooping, he picked it up.

'This proves that there was a woman

here, anyway,' he remarked.

Inspector Bullot came quickly to his side and almost snatched the glove from his hand.

'M'yes.' He looked at it, held it to his nose, sniffed twice, and put it carefully in his pocket. 'We'll go into that later,' he said.

He entered the death room, and following him, Peter watched him from a doorway as he bent over the body.

'H'm! Nasty business!' he muttered, and then looking up quickly: 'You're prepared to identify this as Mr. Slade, the owner of the house?'

'I am,' said Peter. 'There's no doubt about that.'

'You didn't make any examination, I suppose?' The inspector's eyes returned to the body. 'No, of course you didn't. You didn't have time before the lights went out. We must get hold of the police surgeon. I'd like to know approximately what time this man met his death.'

'I can tell you that roughly,' said Peter, and, with the Scotland Yard man's permission, made a hasty examination of the body.

'He hasn't been dead very long,' he announced when he had finished this unpleasant task. 'About an hour and a half.'

'Then it was probably his screams you heard from the drive,' said the inspector, scratching at the grey smear of his moustache. 'It's a queer business — a deuced queer business!'

'Look here!' said Peter, putting into words the curiosity that had been consuming him. 'How did you get here? I mean — how did you know there was anything wrong?'

The inspector looked at him steadily, and it was a long time before he answered.

'That's the queer part of the business, Dr. Lake,' he said at length. 'I don't see any reason why I shouldn't tell you. We were told at Scotland Yard that this crime was going to be committed.'

Peter's face was expressive of his amazement.

'Told?' he repeated blankly.

Inspector Bullot nodded.

'A letter was delivered by special messenger at nine o'clock this evening,' he went on. 'I've got it here.' He put his hand into his breast-pocket and took out a bulky wallet, and from it a single sheet of paper.

The message it contained was type-written and very brief.

To the Cheif Comissioner, New Scotland Yard.

Sir,

If you send someone to 'Five Trees' near Higher Wicklow, the home of Mr. Harvey Slade, at eleven o'clock tonight, they'll find a dead man. The reason for the murder will be worth looking into.

Mr. K.

Peter read the message twice and frowned.

'Who the deuce is 'Mr. K.'?' he asked.

Inspector Bullot refolded the paper and put it back into his pocket-book.

'Who is 'Mr. K.'?' he repeated softly. 'I should very much like to know that, Dr. Lake — I should like to know that very much indeed!'

3

The Seeker

In the narrow grimy streets behind Tottenham Court Road, and farther afield in the slums and alleys of Deptford and Netting Dale, they spoke of Mr. K. with hard eyes and an ugly snarl. None of them had ever seen him, or knew what he looked like, but they all hated him. Tired-eyed and dishevelled women, whose men had been taken away in long police cars, nursed vengeance in their hearts; and convicts in the stone quarries at Dartmoor cursed him below their breath as they worked under the watchful eyes of the warders. For Mr. K. was the king of all 'noses' — a police informer *in excelsis*.

The first of what was destined to be a long series of typewritten slips had reached Scotland Yard eighteen months previously, and concerned one Lew Andronsky, a Polish Jew. There had been a big jewel robbery at a shop in Bond Street. The night watchman had suffered severe injuries to his head and had died in hospital a week later.

There was no clue to the murder until Mr. K.'s neat little letter came into the hands of Inspector Flower. That fat and lethargic official was at first inclined to treat it with the scepticism that such communications deserve, for Scotland Yard looks askance at anonymous letters.

The Assistant Commissioner, however, thought otherwise and ordered that the information should be acted on. He proved to be right, for Lew Andronsky was taken in his sleep at the place mentioned, and sufficient evidence was found in his room to convict him ten times over. Some of the stolen jewellery was discovered, but the bulk never came to light. Andronsky swore that he had parted with it, but he could only give a vague account of where and to whom. According to his story, the man in the car had been masked, and the deal had taken place at the side of a country road late at night. Andronsky was found guilty and duly hanged, his last words as he walked from his cell to the gallows being curses against the unknown squealer who had brought about his downfall.

Al Dane the bank robber, little 'Bud' Smith, Jack Ricketts, and a host of others, in the months that followed, all owed their varying sentences to the information received at Scotland Yard over the signature 'Mr. K.'.

The existence of this mysterious individual leaked out and stirred up bitter resentment among the criminal classes. There was not one of them, from the petty sneak thief to his bigger brother, who would not cheerfully have torn Mr. K. to pieces if they had had the slightest idea who he was. But he kept himself well hidden. Except for his letters to the police he gave no tangible evidence that he was alive. And the police knew no more about him than anyone else. He was nothing: an initial at the foot of a typewritten slip, that was all.

Peter Lake heard most of this from Inspector Bullot and listened in wonderment. The whole thing was so divorced from reality, so like a chapter from the many sensational stories he had read, that he found it difficult to believe — until there came into his vision that sprawling shape by the side of the big desk.

'We tried to telephone the local police here,' said Bullot, 'as soon as we got the letter. But we couldn't get through. The line had been cut a hundred yards away from the station.'

He turned towards the door as the constable and the plainclothes man came in.

'Well?' he asked. 'Found anything?'

'There are traces in a room upstairs on the first landing that bear out Dr. Lake's story about the woman, sir,' said Archer. 'There's an extension telephone up there from the main telephone in the hall, and the wire has been cut.'

'That's where she must have phoned from — ' began Peter, and the inspector nodded sharply.

'It doesn't matter at the moment where she phoned from,' he interrupted. 'Are there any signs of her?'

Archer shook his head.

'No, sir,' he replied. 'There's no woman in this house. There 'as been, though. That room upstairs smells of perfume.'

'We know there has been,' snapped Bullot irritably, 'we've got her glove.'

He frowned and twisted his lower lip between his finger and thumb.

'One of you had better take the car and go and rouse the divisional surgeon,' he said. 'You go, Verney, you know the district. Jackson'll drive you.'

The constable saluted and went out. Bullot, with his brows still drawn together, looked at Peter.

'This man, Slade,' he said. 'Did he live here alone?'

Peter shook his head.

'No,' he answered. 'He had an elderly man and his wife to look after him.'

'Then where are they?' growled Bullot. 'Sure there's nobody in the house except ourselves, Archer?'

'Positive, sir,' replied the plainclothes man.

'Curious,' muttered the inspector. 'Where can they have got to?' He looked at his watch. 'If they'd had the evening off they'd have got back now. It's nearly one.'

Peter began to realize that he was tired, and that the blow on his head had left it aching rather unpleasantly.

'If you don't want me anymore,' he said, 'I'd like to be getting home. I've had quite enough for one evening.'

Bullot looked at him uncertainly, and then nodded grudgingly.

'Yes, I don't think we want you any more at present,' he said. 'We can always find you when we do.'

He began to move about the room, peering at the furniture and fingering the papers on the desk. Peter said good-night, to which the inspector responded with a grunt, and made his way out into the hall. The rain had ceased, but it had cooled the air, and he shivered a little as he walked down the drive. It was very dark, and as he got to the gates leading out into the road he remembered the green fountain pen which he had picked up after his argument with the big man. In the general excitement he had forgotten all about it.

He felt in the jacket pocket into which

he had slipped it, but it was no longer there! He stopped just inside the gates and searched in all his pockets, but there was no sign of the pen. It must have been taken from him while he had been unconscious. He was half-minded to go back and tell the inspector about it, but he was very tired, and weariness won. He would telephone first thing in the morning; delay could make very little difference.

He let himself into his small house with a sigh of relief, and, going into the kitchen, put the kettle on for a cup of tea. While it was boiling he undressed and got into a dressing gown. It seemed to him that a vast amount of time had elapsed since he had set out for the Arlingtons', and yet it was only a matter of a few hours.

He smoked a cigarette while the tea brewed, and was glad to find that his headache had almost gone. The walk home in the cold air had done it good. He drank his tea and went up to bed. His last waking thought as he snuggled his head into the pillow was of the girl whose voice over the telephone had been the introduction to his evening's adventures . . .

He awoke suddenly with an uncomfortable feeling that something was wrong. His training had schooled him into passing from sleep to wakefulness without the usual intermediate state, and he sat up alert and watchful. But no sound greeted his straining ears. What had wakened him? What was now giving him that uneasy feeling that he was no longer alone?

He peered into the darkness, but he could neither hear nor see anything. At his side his watch ticked with apparently unusual loudness, and he was just going to reach over to the little bedside table for it and his torch, which he always kept there, when the gentle pad of feet became audible once more. They ceased and were followed by the rustle of clothes near the foot of the bed.

Cautiously, and without making a sound, Peter reached out for his torch. His fingers closed round it, and bringing it round so that the lens pointed at the spot where he judged the unknown to be,

Peter pressed the button. A blinding sword blade of light cut the darkness and focused on a crouching shape that was bending over the oak chest on which he had put his clothes. Peter heard a startled gasp and a scurry of feet as the surprised burglar made for the door, and then with a single bound he was out of bed. He caught the intruder just as he was vanishing through the door, and dragging him back, reached up and switched on the light.

His captive, a small roughly-clad man with a cloth cap pulled over his eyes, struggled furiously, but he could not break Peter's grip.

'Now,' said Peter grimly, 'let's have a look at you, my friend!'

He jerked off the cloth cap, and then stared in amazement.

The light glinted on golden hair — two wide, frightened eyes looked up at him . . .

'Gosh!' exclaimed Peter, still staring. 'Who are you? What are you doing here?'

The burglar was a girl!

4

The Big Man

The girl stared up at the astonished Peter with an expression of fear and horror, and then with a sudden movement tried to wrench her arm free from his grasp.

'Oh, no, you don't!' breathed Peter softly, and tightened his fingers. 'It's not going to be as easy as that.'

Without letting go his hold he went over to the door, shut it, and turned the key.

'Now,' he said, slipping the key into the pocket of his pyjama jacket, 'we can have a nice quiet little chat.'

He pulled on a dressing gown and perched himself on the side of the bed.

'Sit down,' he went on, nodding towards a chair by the fireplace. 'Make yourself at home.'

'What — what are you going to do?'

The low husky voice was appealing, but

she made no effort to move from her position by the door.

'It's more a question of what you are going to do,' said Peter, and then as she remained silent: 'I think I'm entitled to some sort of an explanation, don't you?'

The wide eyes — he noticed they were of a peculiar shade of blue that was almost violet — flickered uneasily; the tip of a pink tongue slid over scarlet lips, but the girl made no reply.

'You know it's not usual to wake up at half-past three in the morning and find a visitor like you in one's room,' said Peter conversationally; 'in fact, it's distinctly unusual. Who are you, and what's the great idea?'

'Does it matter who I am?'

Her eyes were no longer clouded with fear, but the shakiness of her voice betrayed her unease. Peter, watching her, decided that she was pretty — very pretty — and his interest grew. The rough tweed coat and shapeless flannel trousers she wore enhanced rather than concealed the slimness of her figure. Not at all the kind of burglar one would expect to find in the house at half-past three in the morning.

'I think it matters a lot, under the circumstances,' he said slowly. 'What I really ought to do instead of sitting here talking is to send for the police — '

'Oh, please don't do that!' The frightened look came back to her eyes and her face whitened. 'I've done no harm.'

'Only committed burglary, that's all,' said Peter a little sarcastically. 'A mere nothing.'

She bit her lip and her fingers fumbled with the lapel of her jacket.

'You really are rather cool, you know,' he went on. 'You break into my house, and when you're caught calmly say you've done no harm.'

'Neither have I,' she said quickly, 'I haven't stolen anything. I didn't come to steal anything.'

'Then what did you come for?' he broke in.

She hesitated a moment, and then to Peter's surprise she went over to the chair and sat down.

'I came on a matter of life and death,' she said seriously.

In the pocket of his dressing gown Peter's hand came in contact with a packet of cigarettes. Mechanically he brought it out, put a cigarette between his lips, and reached over to the little table by his bed for the matches.

'I'd like a cigarette, too, please,' said the girl, holding out her hand.

Peter gave her one, found the matches and lit both hers and his own. Sitting once more on the edge of the bed, the humour of the situation suddenly burst on him, and he chuckled.

'What are you laughing at?'

She looked at him wonderingly with the cigarette halfway to her lips.

'I'm laughing because the whole thing strikes me as being funny,' said Peter. 'This is the first time I've enjoyed the thrill of being burgled, and instead of adopting the proper course laid down for all respectable householders and handing the burglar over to the tender mercies of the police, I entertain her with a cigarette.'

She smiled — rather an anaemic attempt, but still a smile. Peter discovered that she had a most attractive dimple at the corner of her mouth.

'You know I'm not a burglar,' she said.

He raised his eyebrows.

'Well, not an ordinary burglar,' she added hastily. 'I'll admit that I've no right to be here.'

'I'm glad you appreciate the enormity of your offence,' said Peter, and this time she laughed outright.

It was a pleasant sound — at least Peter thought so — and added to his mental catalogue of her attractions two rows of small, even and very white teeth.

'I'm afraid I'm too much of a hardened criminal to allow it to weigh very heavily on my conscience,' she retorted.

The fear had gone completely from her eyes, and in its place had appeared a slight twinkle. Peter felt his heart warming towards this girl in spite of the — to say the least of it — unconventional situation in which he had met her. She exhaled a subtle something which for want of a better word, he put down as charm, that made it seem as though he had known her for a very long time.

'Suppose you tell me all about it?' he

suggested. 'The reason for all this, I mean.' He nodded towards her masculine attire. 'I'm presuming, of course, that it's not a habit of yours to walk about dressed like that and break into people's houses.'

'I didn't break in,' she said. 'The kitchen window was open.'

Peter remembered that he had forgotten to perform his usual rounds before going to bed.

'But I take it you don't usually enter people's houses by any window you happen to see open?' he remarked.

She grew suddenly serious.

'No, but on this occasion — as I said — it is a matter of life and death,' she replied. She inhaled deeply at her cigarette, and threw the end into the fireplace. 'I wonder if I can trust you?' she said.

Peter returned her gaze steadily.

'I think you can,' he answered. 'Why not try?'

She was silent for quite a long time, and Peter felt that she was taking stock of him.

'Will you treat what I have to say in strict confidence?' she said at last.

41

He hesitated. Supposing she told him something that it was his duty to pass on to the police? He knew nothing about her, and besides, he felt sure that it was she who had been in that house of death at the time old Harvey Slade had been killed. He had refrained from letting her know it, but he had recognized her voice directly she had spoken as the voice of the girl on the telephone.

She saw his hesitation, and guessed the reason for it.

'I know nothing about the murder,' she said and Peter's face must have expressed his surprise, for she went on: 'Oh, yes, I know you were in the house tonight, and I know what you found there. But I don't know who killed Slade or why he was killed.'

'Do you know 'Mr. K.'?'

The question was past Peter's lips before he could check it, and the effect on the girl was electrical. Her calmness slipped from her like water from a greasy plate. The look of fear came back to her eyes, and she paled to the lips.

'What — what do you know of Mr. K.?'

she breathed huskily.

'Nothing at all,' said Peter. 'I never heard of him until tonight.'

He stopped abruptly and stared at the door. Was it just fancy or had he heard a sound outside in the passage? The girl in the chair followed the direction of his eyes, and her lips parted to speak, but with a quick gesture Peter stopped her and rose to his feet. He had not been mistaken. The handle of the door was softly turning! Somebody outside was trying it to see if it was locked.

In two strides Peter was across the room.

'Who's there?' he called sharply. The answer to his question was startling. There was a sudden crash and the door bulged under the weight of a heavy body!

With a sharp cry the girl sprang to her feet and stood with horrified eyes, her hand at her throat, staring at the creaking wood-work.

'What the hell — ' began Peter angrily, and then, with a splintering, rending sound, the lock gave and the door flew open.

'Don't move, either of you!' snarled a harsh voice and a man came in out of the darkness of the passage.

Peter saw the light glint on the blue nose of an automatic, and his fingers relaxed their grip on the chair he had hastily picked up.

The second visitor of that night was the big man he had nearly knocked out in the drive at 'Five Trees'!

5

Inspector Flower Arrives

The huge figure filled the doorway; a great mountain of living flesh. The abnormally small head set upon a bull neck above the big shoulders swayed gently from side to side like a snake about to strike.

Indeed there was something curiously reptilian about the whole face. The eyes were small and set closely to the round button of a nose; the mouth a twisted red streak that showed up vividly against the grey-white of the skin, was cruel and sensual. On the left cheek — Peter saw this with satisfaction — was a livid bruise.

'Get over there — against the wall.' The voice, devoid now of its previous harshness, was low and gentle like the soft hiss of escaping steam. 'There is a fresh clip of cartridges in this little thing, and if you don't do as I tell you, you'll get them all

— equally divided between you.'

Peter's hands clenched until the nails dug into the palms. A fierce longing to hit this great swollen thing took possession of him, but the sight of the unwavering automatic suggested discretion. It was useless putting up a fight against that. With an almost imperceptible shrug of his shoulders he backed towards the wall the other had indicated.

'That was very wise of you,' said the big man gently. 'Second thoughts are always best. Now,' — he looked from Peter to the terrified girl — 'which of you has it?'

Peter stole a quick glance at his companion. Her eyes were fixed in a stare of horror on the newcomer, and she was breathing in little, short, irregular gasps.

'Come on!' The gentle hissing voice became a snarl. 'One of you has it — which one?'

'Has what?' said Peter.

'The pen!' snapped the big man. 'I had it in my hand when I ran into you in the drive.'

Peter heard the girl draw in her breath sharply, but without taking his eyes off the man with the pistol he said:

'Which pen?'

'The green pen,' said the big man, and his small, beady eyes were full of menace. 'It's no good trying to pretend you don't know what I'm talking about. I know you've got it!'

'Then you know a damn sight more than I do,' said Peter coolly.

The thin lips drew back in a mirthless grin, showing a row of broken discoloured teeth.

'Takin' that line, eh?' he snarled viciously. 'Well, you can cut it out as soon as you like. You've got that pen, and I want it, so hand it over and look slippy about it or it'll be the worse for you!' He waved the muzzle of the automatic threateningly.

'Is it your pen?' asked Peter to gain time, his brain working hastily to find some way out of this unpleasant situation.

'Never mind whose pen it is,' snapped the big man angrily. 'It isn't yours, anyway, and this is none of your business. If you take my advice you'll keep out of it: you know what happened to Harvey Slade?'

'I do,' replied Peter grimly.

'Well,' said the other, 'that's liable to happen again to anyone who butts in on this game.'

'Thanks for the tip,' said Peter. 'Were you responsible for that devilish crime?'

'I wasn't,' said the big man curtly.

Peter looked at him steadily.

'Perhaps it was 'Mr. K.',' he suggested.

A startled expression flashed for a second in the other's face, and then he laughed, a cracked, unpleasant sound that was completely divorced from mirth.

'Perhaps it was,' he answered, 'and perhaps it wasn't. I didn't come here to answer questions, anyhow, and I don't propose to stay here all night, so hand over that pen and I'll go.'

'If you intend stopping until you get that,' said Peter, 'you'll stop here for ever.'

'Oh, will I?' hissed the big man, and his eyes narrowed until they almost completely disappeared. 'We'll see about that.' He advanced two steps and thrust the pistol forward. 'Now,' he grated. 'I'll give you until I count three to hand over that pen, after that I shall shoot!'

'I can save you the trouble of counting

at all,' said Peter calmly. 'I haven't got the pen.'

The face before him twisted into an ugly expression.

'I'm not bluffing — ' began the big man.

'I'm not bluffing either,' snapped Peter. 'I tell you I haven't got the pen.'

'Then what have you done with it?' The small head turned slowly. 'Have you given it to — her?' He looked at the girl balefully.

Peter shook his head.

'What makes you so certain I ever had it?' he asked.

For the first time he saw an expression of doubt come into the other's face.

'I lost it in the drive,' he muttered. 'I know that, and when I went back to look for it it had gone — '

'That may be true,' agreed Peter, 'but it doesn't follow that I was the person who picked it up.'

'You were there — ' began the big man, but Peter interrupted him.

'So were a good many people,' he said. 'The people who slugged me, and afterwards the police!'

'The police!' There was something very like fear in the tone. 'They haven't got it, have they?'

'I don't know who's got it,' said Peter truthfully and a little irritably. 'I only know I haven't. What are you making such a fuss about, anyway? It was only a fountain pen; you can get another exactly like it for ten and sixpence.'

The other took no notice. He seemed to be thinking rapidly.

'Who slugged you?' he asked after a slight pause. 'What was he like?'

'I don't know,' replied Peter. 'If you'd been hit as hard as I was you wouldn't have known either.' And then his anger got the better of him. 'Look here,' he said, 'I'm sick of all these questions, and I'm sick of you and this melodrama stuff. Put that pistol away and clear out.'

The big man's pasty face flushed.

'That's enough of that unless you want to get hurt,' he snarled. 'I'll go when I'm ready and don't forget I've got the whip-hand!' He tapped his pistol meaningfully.

'How do I know that you haven't been lying? How do I know that you haven't got that pen hidden somewhere all the time?'

Peter thought rapidly. How was it possible to turn the tables on this unpleasant adversary?

'Lost your tongue?' snapped the big man impatiently, 'or are you trying to think out some more lies? I know you've got that pen, so why not be sensible and hand it over?'

'Supposing I give you the pen,' said Peter slowly as an idea occurred to him, 'will you clear out?'

The expression of the other's face became eager.

'Directly I get that pen I'll go,' he answered.

'Then I suppose I'd better give it to you,' said Peter with a shrug of his shoulders, and walked over to the oak chest on which his clothes lay.

A startled exclamation came from the girl.

'Don't do that,' she began and the big man swung round on her quickly.

'You shut up!' he snarled and advanced a step towards Peter. 'Come on, hand it over!'

Peter, with his heart beating quickly, picked up his dinner jacket. He made a pretence of feeling in the pocket and then suddenly and without warning flung the jacket full in the big man's face. Taken completely by surprise he staggered back, firing wildly as he did so. The shots, however, whistled harmlessly past Peter and buried themselves in the wall, and the next second he had leaped forward, knocked the gun from the other's hand, and launched himself upon him.

They both crashed heavily to the floor, the big man fighting like a tiger. But Peter was uppermost and held his advantage. With a stream of oaths the other sought for his throat, but Peter gripped his wrists and tore them away. Together they rolled over and over towards the open door and landed with a thud against the jamb. It was Peter's head that came in contact with the wood, and the impact dazed him. His grip loosened, and taking advantage of the fact, the big man threw him off and scrambled to his feet. Before Peter could recover he was running heavily down the passage.

Peter went in pursuit and caught his quarry as he reached the head of the staircase. He dodged a swinging blow to his jaw and retaliated by a short-arm left hook which caught the big man under the heart and made him gasp. The next second he had closed with Peter and they went reeling against the banisters. Peter would easily have got the better of him then, if his foot hadn't slipped. As it was, he lost his balance, and the pair of them went crashing down the staircase to land in a heap in the hall below.

Peter felt the breath leave his body in one enormous gasp as the big man's full weight descended on his stomach. His senses whirled dizzily and as from a long distance he heard an irregular knocking. Dazedly he felt the weight across him suddenly removed, and then, as he recovered his breath, the knocking developed into a thunderous tattoo on the front door.

He heard the thudding of feet and the

bang of a door from the back as he scrambled shakily to his feet and stood leaning against the newel-post. Rat-tat-tat! The knocking came again louder and more insistent. Peter pulled himself together. Who the deuce was this? Some more of them? He hesitated. Perhaps it would be just as well not to open that door. He didn't feel like tackling anybody else at the moment. The knocking was repeated and he heard the rattle of the letter-box as a hand raised the flap.

'Hello, there!' called a deep voice. 'Anything wrong?'

'Who are you?' said Peter, feeling along the wall for the light switch.

'I'm Chief Inspector Flower from Scotland Yard,' answered the voice. 'If that's Dr. Lake I want to see him.'

Peter heard a little gasp of dismay at his elbow, and a hand checked him from turning on the light. The girl had crept down the stairs, and was now standing beside him in the hall.

'Don't open the door — yet,' she breathed in his ear, and as her soft lips brushed his cheek Peter felt an unusual

54

thrill surge through him. She thrust the big man's gun into his hand and then she was gone, leaving behind the faintest trace of an elusive perfume. Against his better judgment Peter let her go.

'All right,' he called to the man outside the door. 'Half a second and I'll let you in.' He waited, pretending to fumble with the chain, until he concluded that the girl had had time to get out through the back, and then switching on the light he opened the door.

A portly figure entered and Peter saw the lights of a small car at the end of the little path by the gate.

Mr. William Flower took in his dishevelled appearance in one apparently lazy glance, and his eyes half closed.

'Dear me, Dr. Lake,' he said gently, 'you appear to have been having a rough time!'

6

Death in the Garden

'A big fat man with a small head,' remarked Mr. Flower slowly. 'H'm! Might almost be a description of me except that I haven't got a small head.' He shook it gently as though to emphasize its size. 'No I can't recollect any known criminal like that. He's a new one on me.'

He was sitting in Peter's shabby little consulting-room sipping the hot tea that at his suggestion Peter had hastily brewed. In the cold grey light of early morning that came in through the window his big heavy face looked old and tired. Peter attributed this to the fact that the stout detective had been up all night, being unaware that it was Mr. William Flower's habitual expression. He had just finished an account of his night's adventures — an account that was true and unembellished, with the exception of one important detail. He had very carefully omitted all mention of the girl in the flannel trousers and sports jacket. Just why he had done this he would have had some difficulty in explaining. Possibly it was just an innate sense of chivalry which is not nearly so dead as the present generation likes to believe.

Mr. Flower gulped down the remains of his second cup of tea and crossed one fat leg over the other.

'This is a funny business all round,' he murmured with a prodigious yawn, balancing the empty cap and saucer on a broad knee. 'A very funny business.'

'It hasn't struck me as particularly humorous,' said Peter dryly.

'Sweet' William — as he was called by his friends and foes alike, partly because of his name, but mostly because of his passion for flowers of all kinds — looked at his new acquaintance with sleepy eyes.

'Hasn't it now?' he said, and his voice sounded a little sorrowful, as though he was rather disappointed. 'Hasn't it? Well, well, p'r'aps we don't look at things in the same way. Now there are several things about this business that strike me as remarkably funny.' He paused, and with an effort set the cup and saucer down on the floor beside his chair. 'I'll tell you some of 'em.'

He settled himself more comfortably with a protesting creak from the chair.

'One,' he went on counting on the fingers of a stubby hand: 'Why did Slade send his servants away? They're not in the house and they haven't come back, so I conclude that he sent 'em away. That's joke number one. Joke number two is, who wrote that letter to the Yard sayin' there was goin' to be a murder?'

'Mr. K., whoever he is,' said Peter.

'No, he didn't,' contradicted the stout inspector decisively, or as near decisively as it was possible for him to get. 'I've seen that letter, an' I've compared it with the others by 'Mr. K.', and I'm willin' to bet he never wrote it.'

'How can you be so certain?' asked Peter. 'It was typewritten — '

'I know it was typewritten,' broke in Mr. Flower. 'Even Bullot could see that. But it wasn't typewritten with the same machine an' it wasn't typewritten on the same paper.'

'I don't see that that's conclusive,' said Peter. 'He could easily have used a different machine and paper.'

Sweet William eyed him pityingly.

'He could but he didn't,' he said gently. 'Because as well as what I've just told you, he spelt 'commissioner' wrong and 'chief' wrong.'

'Yes, I noticed that,' Peter nodded.

'Did you?' said Mr. Flower approvingly. 'Then you're a better detective than Bullot — not that that's much of a compliment. Well, Mr. K. never made a spelling mistake before an' he's always sent his letters to the Chief Commissioner. No, you can take it from me that feller 'K.' never wrote it.'

Peter frowned.

'Why should anyone else write it?' he demanded.

The stout inspector started to shrug his shoulders, found the effort too great, and stopped half-way.

'I don't know for certain,' he answered. 'P'r'aps it was because they wanted to make sure that the police 'ud act on the information, an' p'r'aps it was for another reason.' He suddenly opened his eyes very wide. 'How well did you know this feller Slade?' he asked.

'I didn't know him at all — except by sight,' answered Peter. 'I've seen him once or twice in the village. That's all.'

'H'm!' grunted Sweet William, lapsing once more into his previous lethargic state. 'Well, whoever killed him saved the country a bit o' money.'

Peter looked his surprise.

'What do you mean?' he asked curiously.

'If he hadn't been killed he'd have got fifteen years,' replied Mr. Flower. 'We found enough evidence up at that house to convict him ten times over.'

'Of what?' asked the astonished Peter.

'Fencing and blackmail,' was the laconic answer.

'Great Scott!' exclaimed Peter. 'Old Slade?'

'Old Slade,' repeated the stout man. 'I told you this was a funny business, an' one of the funniest things about it is the girl who phoned you. I'd like to know who she is and why Slade locked her up.'

His eyes sought Peter's as he spoke and they were no longer lazy. Peter shifted uneasily and felt himself flushing. He had an uncomfortable feeling that Mr. Flower was aware that the girl had been there that night.

'She couldn't have had anything to do with the murder,' he said hastily. 'Slade was alive when he locked her in — '

'He was alive when he locked her in,' said Sweet William, 'but was he alive when somebody let her out?' He was still watching Peter steadily. 'Somebody let her out, you know. She couldn't have got out by the window because it was screwed up, an' she couldn't have turned the key herself because it was on the outside of the door. An' she wasn't there when Bullot arrived, so I deduce that somebody let her out.'

He waited, but Peter remained silent.

'Did the somebody who let her out kill Slade,' Mr. Flower went on, 'or was Slade already dead when the somebody arrived? It's all very interestin' and the most interestin' thing about it is why that feller who came here is so anxious about that green pen.' He nodded several times, and then went off at a tangent. 'Do you use scent, Dr. Lake?'

The question took Peter completely by surprise. It was so unexpected.

'Er — no — why?' he stammered.

'Thought I smelt scent when I came in,' said Mr. Flower. 'If you don't use it it must have been my imagination. Imagination's one of my strong points. I'm always imagining things. F'rinstance, this scent I thought I smelt was just like the scent that girl left behind in that room at 'Five Trees.''

So he knew, thought Peter in dismay; knew that the girl had been there that night in spite of the fact that he hadn't mentioned it. The sleepy-looking eyes and lazy manner were just a blind concealing a particularly alert brain. Still Peter decided he had no direct proof, and he wasn't going to be trapped into admitting that the girl had been there.

'Your imagination must be very vivid indeed,' he said as coolly as he could. 'I can't smell any scent.'

'I can't — now,' said the stout inspector and hoisted himself with difficulty to his feet. 'What sort of a garden have you got here?' he asked.

Peter was getting a little bewildered at these sudden changes of subject.

'Nothing very much,' he answered.

'I'd like to see it,' said Mr. Flower. 'I'm fond of gardens. Horticulture's my hobby. Besides, that big feller, when he escaped, may have left some interestin' traces.'

He moved over to the door, and Peter followed puzzling over the reason for the sudden desire to view his small scrap of land. He did not believe for a moment that the detective's explanation was the real one. Leading the way along the passage and through the tiny kitchen he opened the back door.

'There you are,' he said. 'There's the garden, such as it is.'

Mr. Flower looked slowly about him.

'Could be made very nice with a little trouble,' he remarked. 'Those rose trees want prunin' another year. You'd get better blooms. So this was the way that feller went — along that path and through the little gate?' He dropped his eyes to the wet gravel at his feet, and shook his head. 'Curious,' he said, 'you never told me he was wearin' ladies' shoes!'

Peter followed the direction of his eyes and saw the clear print of a dainty shoe — the cause of Mr. Flower's remark. So that was why he had been so interested in the garden. He had guessed that if the girl had been there she would leave this way and had hoped to find confirmation of her presence.

'I — ' began Peter, and discovered he was speaking to empty air. With surprisingly quick strides for one of his size, Mr. Flower was moving swiftly down the path in the direction of the small gate at the end of the garden.

Peter frowned, and went after him wondering what had so suddenly interested him. Halfway along the path he saw.

Near the gate was a thick bank of evergreens, and projecting from the massed foliage — a foot!

It was a large foot, and with a rapidly beating heart Peter broke into a run. As he came level with Mr. Flower the stout man stooped, and parted the screening branches. The green of the leaves was splashed and mottled with red, and Peter saw the reason as he gazed down at the huddled form that lay in their midst.

It was the big man, and he had died in the same way that Harvey had died — horribly, stabbed in the throat!

7

The Warning!

The man seated at the wheel of the motionless car looked anxiously along the wide stretch of country road dimly visible in the grey of the dawn, and cursed softly below his breath. He was feeling cold and stiff, huddled up among his rugs in the shadowy recesses of the limousine.

Presently the man at the wheel — a little wizened fellow with a yellow pock-marked face, yawned, stretched himself, and producing a cheap packet of cigarettes, lighted one. He inhaled the smoke gratefully, and turning slid back a window in the glass partition that separated the driving-seat from the interior of the car.

''Ow much longer d'you think Ledder's going ter be, guv'nor?' he asked, peering through the square aperture.

The man addressed grunted and raised his head.

'How should I know?' he snapped irritably. 'The fool ought to have been back by now.'

'P'r'aps he's 'ad trouble,' said the little man apprehensively.

'Ledder's capable of taking care of himself,' growled the other.

'Bit o' bad luck 'is runnin' up against the chap in the drive,' muttered the pock-marked man. 'If 'e 'adn't done that we'd a got what we was after and bin away by now.'

'It was cursed bad management on Ledder's part,' retorted the man in the car. 'If the sight of old Slade lying there dead hadn't scared him he'd have been more careful.'

His companion shivered.

'I was scared too,' he admitted candidly. 'An' I only 'eard the scream. Blimey! It was awful, wasn't it?'

The thin lips of the man behind him curled into a contemptuous sneer.

'It didn't upset me,' he replied.

'Nuthin' 'ud upset you,' said the little man with grudging admiration. 'You ain't got no nerves, guv'nor.'

'I've got nerves, but I know how to control them, Biker,' was the reply. 'It would take more than a scream and the sight of a dead man to scare me into a panic.'

Biker relapsed into silence, puffing at his cigarette.

'I wonder 'oo killed the old beggar?' he said thoughtfully at last.

The thin shoulders of the other hunched into a shrug.

'Does it matter?' he snapped harshly. 'Whoever it was, he saved me the trouble. Nothing but death would have parted Slade from his precious pen.'

'I 'ope Ledder's succeeded in gettin' it,' said Biker. 'Ter think 'e 'ad it in 'is 'and and then lost it!' He stopped as a thought struck him. ''Ere, I say,' he went on, his voice suddenly shrill with anxiety. 'Yer don't think 'e's got it and 'e's goin' off with it on his own, do you? He's bin a 'ell of a long time — '

'He wouldn't dare.' The words were confident, but the tone of the voice suggested a slight doubt. 'He wouldn't dare try and double-cross me.'

'Ledder 'ud double-cross the h'angel Gabriel if 'e thought 'e was goin' to get enough out of it,' declared Bilter. 'An' don't you make no mistake.'

The heavy brows of the man in the back drew down over the bridge of his thin pendulous nose. There was something vulture-like about him as he sat there half-crouched in the corner, thinking over the startling suggestion that his companion had put forward.

'I don't think Ledder would risk it even though the prize is a high one,' he said at length. 'He knows me too well, and he knows that if he did that I'd get him wherever he went.'

Biker threw away the stub of his cigarette.

'Well I wish 'e'd 'urry up that's all,' he said. 'I'm cold and I'm tired and I'm sick of sittin' 'ere.'

'I'm tired too, but I'm not making a fuss about it,' snarled the other. 'You want to live on a bed of roses.'

'There ain't bin no bed nor roses about tonight,' grumbled the little man. 'Me 'eart's in me mouth most of the time.'

'I wish it was there no,' grated his companion. 'Perhaps it would stop you talking. Shut up and shut that window. There's an infernal draught.'

Biker opened his mouth to reply, thought better of it, slammed the sliding window to, and huddled himself up as comfortably as he could in his seat.

The man inside the car drew his rugs closer around and stared out of the side window at the rapidly lightening landscape.

To judge by his face his thoughts were not pleasant ones, for every now and again he scowled and his lips compressed until they were almost invisible in the grey of his face. It was an evil face, lined and scored, and greed showed in the furrows about the nostrils and mouth. And yet the man could not have been so very old for the hair — such of it as could be seen under the broad brim of the soft hat he wore — was jet black.

The minutes passed and presently he stirred, fumbled in his breast pocket and produced a cigar-case. Selecting a cigar and biting off the end with a set of peculiarly white and even teeth, he settled back once more in his corner.

It was Bilter who first heard the sound of the car engine. On the still air of the morning it came with remarkable clearness long before the car itself was visible, and it woke Biker from a gentle doze.

He sat up looking along the ribbon of road that stretched ahead with narrowed eyes. He saw the car come round the bend, and noticed that it was travelling at good speed.

The sound of the exhaust grew louder, and he saw that the machine was a long low racer, painted black. There was only one occupant, a solitary figure crouched over the wheel.

Without a great deal of interest Bilter watched the car draw nearer, but he suddenly became alert as the low humming roar of the engine dwindled when it was a hundred yards away and the machine began to slow down. With an oath he swung himself out of the driving seat and dropped on to the roadway as the black car slid alongside the standing limousine and came to a halt.

'Stay where you are and don't trouble to pull that gun,' ordered a high-pitched voice, and Biker, whose hand had gone instinctively to his hip pocket, found himself staring blankly into the muzzle of an automatic held in the gloved hand of the driver.

'I'm a very good shot,' continued the voice, 'so I don't advise you to take any risks. If I have to shoot I shall shoot to kill.'

'What do you want?' began Biker hoarsely.

'I want to speak to your employer,' interrupted the man with the gun. 'Open the door and tell him to get out.'

With one eye on the gun Biker moved to obey, but was saved the trouble, for the window slid down and the scowling face of the man inside was thrust through the aperture.

'What's all this?' he demanded harshly.

'Good morning, Mr. Paul Andronsky,' greeted the man in the black car pleasantly. 'I've just come along to save you wasting your time.'

The face of the man addressed as

Andronsky went grey, and there was a flicker of fear in his eyes as he stared at the leather-covered head and goggled eyes of the other.

'Who are you?' he stammered. 'What do you mean?'

'Your brother knew me as 'Mr. K.', and that's as good a name as any other,' answered the goggled man calmly.

'Mr. K!' Paul Andronsky's lean jaw dropped, and the fear in his eyes deepened to sheer terror. Biker, his eyes almost starting from his head, muttered a strangled oath.

Mr. K. took no notice of the sensation he had caused.

'Lew Andronsky tried to play me up,' he went on still in the same high-pitched obviously disguised voice, 'and for that he went to the gallows. Al Dane, Bud Smith, and Jack Ricketts tried the same game, and they, too, suffered in varying degrees.'

Paul Andronsky's face flushed, changing from unhealthy grey to an unpleasant liver colour.

'You darned squealer!' he snarled thickly.

'Not at all,' said the man in the black car coolly. 'I merely used the law to punish them instead of doing so myself, and I can assure you that the law was more lenient than I should have been. But I'm not going to waste time, either discussing or justifying my methods.' His voice changed and there was a menacing note in it that sent a cold shiver through the two men he was addressing: 'Keep out of this Slade business, Andronsky, I know what you're after but you won't get it — neither will Ledder. That green pen, when it's found, belongs to me. I don't know who's got it at the moment, but when I find out it will be the worse for them.'

His left hand came up out of the car with a throwing motion, and something fell at Biker's feet.

'It's no good waiting for Ledder,' he said. 'He won't come back — perhaps you can guess why.'

He pressed his foot on the accelerator, and the long black car shot forward and roared away up the road. As the sound of its engine grew less Bilter stooped and picked up the thing at his feet.

'Blimey!' he breathed huskily, and his

face was chalk white, for between his shaking fingers was a long-bladed knife, and the steel was wet with blood. He looked at Paul Andronsky, but neither asked whose blood it was — they both knew!

8

Peter Gets Another Shock

To Peter Lake the three hours following the discovery of the body of the big man were like a particularly unpleasant nightmare. His small house literally buzzed with policemen. Inspector Bullot, hastily summoned, arrived breathlessly, held a hurried conference with Mr. William Flower, left behind a local inspector and a constable and departed in a whirl of officialdom. The police surgeon, a man from the neighbouring town, came just before the ambulance. He was a brusque man with a staccato manner of speech, and Peter, who had never seen him before, took an instant and intense dislike to him. He rather grudgingly confirmed Peter's diagnosis of the cause of death, promised to drop his report into the station during the morning, and went away with the ambulance and all that remained of the big man.

'He was murdered by the same man who murdered Slade,' said Mr. William Flower, puffing at an evil-smelling black cigar, which he had extracted from one of the pockets of his capacious waistcoat. 'There's no doubt about that. The two killings are identical, except that in Slade's case he left the knife behind.'

'Who was the dead man? Did you find out?' asked Peter, and the stout inspector nodded.

'He was a man called Ledder,' he answered. 'Beyond that I don't know anything about him, but it won't be very long before I know all about him. There was a letter in his pocket, with his name and address on it, and I'm havin' inquiries made.' He rolled the cigar from one corner of his mouth to the other. 'About this green pen, Dr. Lake,' he went on, 'are you quite certain that the person who 'coshed' you took it?'

'Well, I had it in my pocket at the time, and I hadn't got it after,' said Peter, 'so it seems pretty obvious.'

'H'm!' remarked Sweet William, staring

at a corner of the ceiling. 'Ledder couldn't have known that, or he wouldn't have taken the trouble to come along here after it. It looks as though more than one person was interested in that pen.'

Peter could have assured him definitely on this point, but he kept his mouth shut. Throughout the questions that had been fired at him that morning he had been dreading that Mr. Flower would revert to the presence of the girl and demand an explanation for that tell-tale footprint on the gravel. He had even been at some pains to think up a good one, but the dreaded question never came. Mr. Flower had apparently forgotten all about the footprint in the stress of more important things.

Again and again, Peter told himself that he was a fool, and something more than a fool to worry about a girl of whom he knew nothing, and had only seen once in his life, and then under circumstances that wanted a lot of explaining.

By suppressing evidence that might be helpful to the police he was laying himself open to a grave charge. The punishment for an accessory after the fact in murder was no light one, and he was risking all this for a pretty face that dimpled rather nicely when it smiled. No, that was not quite true. There was something more in it than that; something about the girl's personality that had reached out and found an answering something in his own. That was the only way he could describe it, and although his brain told him that he was acting like a fool, he could no more have followed its suggestion than he could have flown.

Instinct, which is older, and in certain circumstances, stronger than reason, had the upper hand.

Mr. Flower took his departure at last, leaving Peter hollow-eyed from his sleepless night, to sit down to a frugal lunch prepared by the woman, who came in daily to 'do for him' and sometimes nearly did.

He was just finishing his meal when George Arlington arrived. A tall, readily-smiling man of thirty-six, he radiated cheerfulness.

'What's all this I hear?' he greeted,

dropping into a chair and lighting a cigarette. 'Battle, murder and sudden death let loose in the village. Tell me all about it.'

Peter swallowed a final mouthful of bread and cheese.

'I'll tell you nothing, George,' he said. 'I'm sick of the whole thing.'

His friend eyed him sympathetically.

'Had a gruelling time of it, have you?' he murmured. 'You don't look up to much, but you must make an effort, old man. Here's a first-class sensation with you as the central figure, and I'm longing to hear all the gory details.'

Peter groaned and pushed back his chair from the table.

'How did you hear anything about it?' he said.

Arlington smiled — a curious smile that ran up one side of his face, leaving the other in repose.

'I am the possessor of a servant,' he replied, 'who is better at dishing out news than any newspaper. I heard all about the business at breakfast.'

'Then why come and bother me?'

demanded Peter impolitely.

'Because you are in possession of the inside information,' retorted his friend. 'Now, come on, spill the beans, and let's hear all about it.'

'Give me a cigarette, then,' said Peter, valiantly trying to suppress a yawn and failing. 'You're a beastly old slave-driver, George.'

Arlington grinned and gave him a cigarette, and Peter, after a preliminary puff, began his story.

His audience was an attentive one, for he listened without interruption. When Peter had finished he pursed his lips and whistled.

'By Jove, it's a mysterious business!' he remarked. 'I wonder what happened to the girl?'

Peter hesitated. He had half a mind to tell his friend about the girl's visit, but he thought better of it, and shook his head.

'I couldn't tell you,' he said, easing his conscience with the reflection that this was strictly true.

'It seems to me,' Arlington continued, 'that it's damned lucky for you that you did lose that pen, or have it pinched. Rather unhealthy to have it in one's possession apparently.' He flicked the end of his cigarette into the fireplace. 'I'd like to know why that fellow — what's his name — '

'Ledder,' said Peter and Arlington nodded. 'I'd like to know why he was so keen to get hold of it.'

'So would the police,' said Peter. 'There must be something concealed in that pen of considerable value.'

'I agree with you.' Arlington wrinkled his brows thoughtfully. 'You say this man Slade was a fence? Perhaps he was a miser as well, and the pen shows where he's hidden his money?'

Peter was too tired to offer any suggestions. His eyes felt hot and heavy, through lack of sleep, and he wished George Arlington to Jericho. But George was full of ideas and theories, and he recounted these at great length until Peter could cheerfully have killed him.

However, he went at last, after extricating a promise from Peter to keep him posted with all the latest developments and Peter dragged his weary body upstairs to his bedroom. Dressed as he was he flung himself on the bed, and with a sigh of relief buried his aching head in the cool pillow.

It must have been late when he awoke, for it was quite dark outside, and, looking at his watch, he saw that the time was nearly eleven. But his long sleep had done him good. After a cold bath he went downstairs feeling as fit as a fiddle and ravenously hungry.

He was rummaging about in the pantry in search of food when he thought he heard a sound at the back door. Going out into the little scullery, he stood listening. The sound came again; irregular sobbing breathing, and this time it was accompanied by a frantic scrabbling on the panels.

In two strides Peter was at the door. Pulling back the bolt, he turned the handle, and then, as the door swung open, something fell heavily into his arms. With an exclamation of alarm and surprise, he found himself looking down into the unconscious face of the girl of the previous night!

9

Lola Marsh's Secret

She lay limply in his arms breathing heavily and at first Peter was afraid that she had been hurt. A second rapid glance, however, reassured him. She had only fainted.

He carried her into the consulting room, laid her down on the shabby little settee, and set to work to bring her round. In a few seconds his efforts were rewarded, for she opened her eyes. He saw the wild fear in them, as she started up, and laid a soothing hand on her shoulder.

'Keep still for a bit,' he said. 'You're quite safe.'

The terror faded from her face, and as he slipped a cushion behind her head she sank back against it with a little sigh. Peter stood looking down at her in silence, and thought he had never seen anything more lovely. She was dressed this time in a severely-cut costume of black face-cloth, and the sombre hue brought out all the beauty of her hair and skin. The small black hat she had been wearing he had taken off, and realizing that he was still holding it, he set it down on the table. Turning back again, he saw that she was watching him solemnly.

'Feeling better?' he asked.

She nodded.

'What happened?' he went on. 'Something frightened you. What was it?'

A shadow of the fear he had seen before returned to her eyes.

'It was the man in the drive,' she said in a low voice, and shivered.

Peter stared.

'The man in the drive?' he repeated. 'Which drive?'

'The drive at 'Five Trees',' she answered.

'What in the world were you doing there at this time of night?' said Peter in amazement.

'I was going to the house,' she replied simply and without hesitation, 'and half-way up the drive I ran into him. He had on a leather helmet and goggles, and he started to chase me. I was horribly frightened, and I ran and ran until I found myself near your gate. I thought I'd be safe here — '

Peter ran his fingers through his hair.

'Look here,' he suggested. 'Suppose you tell me all you know about this extraordinary business. It all seems quite mad to me. I'm like a man who has gone into a theatre in the middle of a play and gets in half-way through the second act. I don't know the plot, and,' — he looked at her meaningfully — 'I don't know the names of the characters.'

'I don't know them all,' she said with a faint smile that brought out the dimple again, 'but my name's Lola Marsh, if that's what you mean.'

'That was partly what I meant, thank you,' said Peter, and went on quickly: 'I don't want to butt in on something that doesn't concern me, but if there's anything I can do I'd like to help.'

The violet blue eyes softened.

'That's rather nice of you, Dr. Lake,' she murmured, 'particularly after what

— after what we did to you.' She saw the bewilderment in his face, and went on quickly: 'It was Jim, my brother, who — who hit you last night at 'Five Trees'.'

'Oh, was it?' said Peter grimly.

'He didn't know it was you,' said Lola hastily. 'I mean we thought you were one of the others.'

'I see,' said Peter, and frowned. 'So it wasn't you or your brother who took that green pen out of my pocket?'

She shook her head.

'Of course it wasn't,' she said. 'Otherwise I shouldn't have come here last night to try and get it. Did you think it was?'

'I naturally thought it was the person who coshed me,' said Peter, 'because I don't see who else had the chance.'

'Somebody may have come in while you were still unconscious — after we had gone,' she suggested, and Peter nodded.

'That seems to be a possible explanation,' he agreed. 'What is there about this pen that makes it so valuable?'

She hesitated.

'It's rather a long story — ' she began.

'Never mind how long it is,' interrupted

Peter. 'If you're willing to tell me I'm only too anxious to listen.'

For a moment she was silent, and then, apparently making up her mind, she said:

'I think I'd better begin by telling you that I was Harvey Slade's secretary.'

Peter looked at her in amazement. This was the last thing he had expected.

'You look surprised,' she said with a faint smile. 'Yes, I was his secretary, if you could call my position by such a name.' She paused a moment, frowned, and then went on: 'Harvey Slade was a fence, and I used to smuggle the stuff that came into his possession out of the country.'

She watched him to see the effect of this declaration, but although it was something of a shock, Peter managed to return her gaze without blinking.

'Go on,' he said quietly.

'I didn't know what I was doing at first,' she continued. 'In fact, I wasn't sure until six months ago. I first began to get suspicious when he doubled my salary — I was getting quite a big one before — and then as though that were not enough, he began giving me an extra hundred pounds every time I crossed the Channel for him. Knowing his meanness in other things it struck me as strange he should be so generous. It took me some time to find out just how wickedly clever the whole plot was — and then I only found out by accident. The things I used to take across to Antwerp were old books — first editions. There was an old Dutchman — Shwietzer, his name was — who kept a book store, and I had to deliver the books to him. He paid me in cash, English money, which I brought back to Slade.'

'And do you mean that the stolen stuff was concealed in the books?' exclaimed Peter.

She nodded.

'Yes, but oh, so cleverly! It was jewellery, of course — single stones without their settings — and they were concealed in the bindings where the pages are fixed into the back of the book. You could open the books without discovering anything. Wasn't it clever? You see, the Customs people are not very particular going into the country, and the books were genuine first editions, and some of them were worth quite a lot of money.'

'But,' said Peter, 'when you found out what you were really doing, why didn't you go to the police?'

She looked at him queerly.

'When I've finished you'll understand,' she said. 'I told you I found out the real nature of what I was doing by accident. I had been given a book to take over one day which rather interested me. It was full of old woodcuts, and instead of packing it up in my little office at once, which I usually did, I thought I'd look through it. While I was doing so I felt something hard in the back, and discovered half a dozen large diamonds.

'At first I was puzzled, and should still have been if Harvey Slade hadn't come in at the moment and caught me. As soon as I saw him I guessed that there was something wrong about those diamonds. His face was dreadful. For a horrible moment I thought he was going to reach out and strangle me. Then he closed the door and locked it, and came over to me. 'So, Miss Inquisitive, you've found the secret out, have you?' he said quietly, and then he told me the truth.'

'I still don't see why you didn't go to the police,' said Peter, shaking his head. 'It was the obvious thing to do.'

'I threatened to do so at first,' she replied, 'but Slade only laughed at me and then showed me just how I stood. He had letters and papers that would have satisfied any judge that I was a party to the business; and that I was actually taking my share of the proceeds. Do you see the wicked cleverness of it? That raised salary, the extra hundred pounds every trip I took. He had made me sign a receipt for each one. Would any living jury believe that I was getting a hundred pounds in addition to my salary for taking a parcel of old books across the Channel? And there were letters too. Letters written to Shwietzer explaining who I was and saying that I was perfectly conversant with all matters in which I was dealing. And I had made the journey twenty or thirty times. The Customs people knew me well. Not a living soul would ever have believed for one moment that I was innocent.'

'Great Scott! What a ghastly plot!' muttered Peter as he realized that what she said was true. Nobody would believe her. And then an idea occurred to him. 'But Slade's dead now,' he said. 'You're safe enough now.'

'Am I?' she answered bitterly. 'Don't you see that those letters and receipts are still in existence, and if they get into the hands of the police — '

'By Jove! I never thought of that,' said Peter blankly.

'I begged Slade to give them back to me,' said Lola. 'I offered him most of the money he had given me to let me destroy those letters and receipts and let me go, but he only laughed at me. And he still forced me to go on taking those books across to Amsterdam. Last night he wanted me to go again, and he got angry when I refused and locked me in my office.'

'So you saw nothing of the murder?' said Peter.

'No,' she answered. 'I only heard him scream. I had arranged to ring up my brother and when I didn't, he came to the house and arrived in time to let me out.'

She shuddered.

There was a short silence, and then Peter asked suddenly:

'Who is 'Mr. K.'?'

'He is the man who used to come and see Slade,' she answered. 'But who he is I don't know. He always wore goggles and a leather motoring helmet, and he never came unless the servants had been sent out. He was there tonight — lurking in the drive — '

'When you went to try and find those letters?' Peter hazarded.

'Yes,' she said. 'It was a forlorn hope. I had little chance of being able to find them without the pen.'

'The pen?' echoed Peter, momentarily puzzled, and she explained.

'Somewhere in 'Five Trees' there's a secret safe. I think it's hidden somewhere in the study, but I'm not sure. You see Slade never had a banking account. He kept all his money on the premises.'

'And the pen contains the secret of this safe?' asked Peter.

She nodded.

'I think so,' she answered. 'Once — months ago — I saw Slade scribble something on a piece of paper and put it inside the cap of the pen.'

So that was it. Peter understood now why the big man, Ledder, had been so anxious to get the green pen back in his possession. It held the key to a fortune — the accumulated wealth from old Harvey Slade's illegal trading, and also those papers incriminating Lola Marsh.

Peter's brows drew down over his eyes thoughtfully. He had offered to help — he wanted very badly to help. How could he?

'You were taking a pretty big risk going to 'Five Trees' weren't you?' he said abruptly. 'The servants must be back by now — '

'They came back but they wouldn't stay after they heard what had happened,' she said. 'They've got a room at the village inn until after the inquest.'

'So there's nobody at 'Five Trees'.' Peter made the statement, and at the same time came to his decision. 'Miss Marsh, I'm going to have a shot at finding that safe — tonight — and if the person who pinched that pen from me hasn't got there first, I'll try and bring those letters back to you.'

10

The Man in the Mask

Two o'clock struck on the cracked bell of the little village church and the reverberations were caught up by the wind and whirled away to silence. The solitary constable on guard at the drive gates at 'Five Trees' shivered. With the coming of darkness the temperature had fallen and although the wind was little more than a breeze, it was cold.

The man stood at the gates and looked down the silent stretch of road for a sight of his relief. He had done his rounds. Lola Marsh, although she hadn't known it, had had a lucky escape, for this policeman had been round at the back when she had come up the drive, and but for her meeting with Mr. K she would most certainly have encountered him.

Presently as he stood there, he saw his relief come plodding up the road, a lighted cigarette between his lips.

'All right, Jack?' asked the newcomer as he came up to his companion.

'All quiet on the Western Front,' grinned Jack. 'Not a darned thing stirring and not a soul about. 'S'nough ter give yer the creeps. Whoever picked this 'ouse for a murder picked a right one.' He tucked his rolled-up cape under his arm and prepared to depart. 'Well, you've got it for the next eight hours — and you're welcome to it. Good night, mate.'

He went striding off down the road, little thinking that his casual good night was really goodbye, and that he was destined never to see the man who had relieved him alive again.

As his footsteps faded away, a great and somehow ominous silence settled down again over the darkness.

The constable who had remained behind squinted over his shoulder into the shadows of the driveway. All was black and silent. There was a lull in the wind and not even the great trees that flanked the borders rustled. He grunted and threw away his cigarette. Duty was duty and he had to do it, however unpleasant the task.

Switching on his flashlamp, he went quietly up the drive towards the house. As he disappeared, a shadow, black on the blackness of the high hedge on the other side of the roadway, broke away from its shelter and stealing across was swallowed up in the darkness of the drive.

With his heart beating faster than was its wont, Peter Lake stole cautiously along the grass border towards the dimly-seen bulk of the house. He had had great difficulty in persuading Lola Marsh to let him undertake his mission, but he had succeeded in insisting that the girl should wait for him until he came back. And he had reached 'Five Trees' in time to see the constable at the gates.

It had given him something of a shock, for he had not reckoned on the place being guarded, and his first thought had been to give up the venture. And then the thought of going back to the girl and confessing failure after all, had urged him on and he had decided to risk it. In any case, it was going to be difficult for he realized now that he was actually on the spot, that even if he found Harvey Slade's hidden safe, it would be next to impossible to open it.

But Peter was an optimist and a great believer in luck. He had read somewhere that a combination safe could be opened by listening for the fall of the tumblers as the dial was turned, and he had brought a stethoscope with him.

Reaching the top of the drive, he waited in the concealment of the shrubbery for the return of the constable and presently he saw his dancing light. The man passed him at barely three yards distance, and two minutes later Peter was creeping in at the dining room window. Without making a sound, he closed the sash behind him and slipped the catch. For some seconds, he stood motionless in the stillness of that house where death in the guise of murder had paid so recent a visit, and then he felt his way out into the hall.

He remembered the position of the study door, and crept towards it. It was shut, but he turned the handle and entered the room.

He had provided himself with a torch, over the lens of which he had stuck some black court-plaster with a hole in the centre just sufficiently large to allow a pencil of light to shine through. He fumbled for this now, and switching it on, sent the narrow beam travelling slowly over the room. Not a thing had been moved in that place of death. Only in one way was the room different — and Peter noticed the difference with thankfulness. That sprawling thing by the desk had been removed.

He closed the door and going over to the windows pulled the heavy curtains across so that no chance gleam from his masked torch should warn the constable outside of an unlawful presence within. And then he began his search.

He started with the walls, examining them inch by inch, and every now and again tapping at the panelling with his knuckles. But they yielded nothing. No hollow sound rewarded his diligence. By the time he had completed a circuit of the room, Peter was both puzzled and disappointed. For some reason best known to himself he had expected to find the hidden safe in those panelled walls. If it was in the room at all, it was the natural place one would expect to find it.

But was it in the room, and what was more, did it exist? Had the girl allowed her imagination to get the better of her? After all she had no proof. It was only an idea based on the fact that old Harvey Slade hadn't possessed a banking account. She had nothing more tangible to go on than that. And yet, of course, when he came to think of it she was right.

Dealing in stolen jewellery as he had, Slade must have had some place to keep it. He couldn't leave it lying about the room or trust to the flimsy drawers of a desk. The desk! Perhaps there was something there that would give him the clue he was seeking.

Peter went over to the massive piece of furniture and pulled open a drawer. It was empty. He soon discovered that the rest of the drawers were in a like condition. Of course, he might have expected it. The police had taken all the contents for examination.

He went cold as he thought that those papers incriminating the girl might be among them. But, of course, they hadn't been. If they had, she would have been arrested by now. It suddenly struck him that in any case they must know her identity by now. The servants would have given her name and description to them.

Well, so long as those papers did not come to light, she was all right; but how the devil was he to find them?

He stood in the middle of the room and thought. And then from, outside, he heard the soft crunch of approaching footsteps. The constable was coming round again on his second circuit of the house.

Peter switched out his torch, and waited tensely in the dark for the man to finish his rounds and go back to his lonely vigil by the gate.

The footsteps came on, steady and ponderous. Peter heard him rattle the handle of the back door and pass on. Round the side or the house came the measured tread, and then, immediately outside the window, it suddenly stopped.

Peter heard a low exclamation and his

heart leaped into his mouth. Why had the man stopped? What had he seen? And then he realized, in a sudden burst of enlightenment. Of course, the curtains!

When the man had been round before they had been open; now his flashlamp had shown him that they were drawn. He knew that somebody was inside the house; somebody who had no right to be there. Peter felt his hands go sticky as he waited there listening. If he were caught he would have a hard job to explain his presence.

What should he do?

Wait by the front door and make a dash for it when the constable came in? Wait where he was and get out by the window as soon as the man moved away? Or try to get out by the back?

It depended which way the policeman went when he moved.

He strained his ears but no sound came now from outside. Guessing that something was wrong the constable was not advertising his movements.

An eternity seemed to pass and still there was silence — complete unbroken silence. Peter felt the sweat break out on his forehead. What was the man doing out there?

At last he could stand it no longer, and making up his mind he crept out into the hall. If the constable came that way he could dash past him in the darkness, and if he came the other way, he would hear him and still make his escape by the front door. He reached the hall and stopped to listen again. This time he heard something — the crunch of a footstep on the gravel. So the constable was coming that way, was he? Pressing himself against the wall, he waited; his muscles tense. There came the click of metal against metal warning him that a key was turning in the lock. He braced himself for the rush as a breath of cool air fanned his heated face, and then, with a sudden blaze, the hall lights came on.

Peter's breath left his lungs in a gasp of sheer astonishment, for instead of the constable, there stood on the threshold a tall, gaunt figure, clad entirely in black, whose malevolent eyes stared at him menacingly through the slits in the mask that concealed his face!

11

Danger!

The man in the mask stood motionless, one gloved hand on the electric light switches, the other gripped round the butt of a wicked-looking automatic, and the astonished Peter gave a little shiver as he looked at this unexpected apparition, for the half-glimpsed eyes were evilly malignant.

'Well,' snarled a harsh voice. 'What are you doing here?'

There was a curious intensity about that voice. It was low and oddly distinct, with a quality of hard sibilance about it that was as penetrating as a bullet.

Peter stared at the masked face and kept silent. Without shifting his eyes from Peter's face the masked man advanced a couple of paces, and closed the door.

'You, I suppose, are Dr. Lake?' he said thoughtfully.

'Your supposition is right,' replied Peter, recovering a little from his first shock of surprise. 'May I ask who you are?'

'You may ask,' answered the other, 'but I shan't answer. It is no concern of yours who I am.'

'I see,' said Peter pleasantly, but his eyes narrowed. 'Well, I should put away that gun if I were you and clear out. Perhaps you don't know it, but there's a constable outside, and I don't think it will be very long before he's inside.'

The masked man shrugged his shoulders.

'That is where you are wrong,' he retorted. 'There *was* a constable outside. I have been watching him for quite a while. I can assure you, however, that he will not interfere.'

Peter went suddenly cold.

'You mean — ' he cried hoarsely.

'I mean,' said the other quickly, 'that he is no longer in a position to take any further interest in the proceedings. It is quite remarkable how chloroform affects people like that.' His voice changed, and became tense and menacing. 'Now, Dr. Lake, without wasting further time, where is that pen?'

Peter frowned. So here was another one after the pen.

'I haven't the least idea,' he replied steadily.

'You haven't the least idea?' repeated the black-clad figure softly. 'Then what are you doing here?'

Peter tried to think of a convincing answer to this question, failed and said nothing.

'Come, come, Dr. Lake,' snapped the masked man impatiently. 'If you have no knowledge of the green pen — if you do not know of its significance — why are you in this house at so late an hour?'

'That is my business,' said Peter.

'You'll find that it's mine also,' snarled the other. 'Stop being a fool and give me that pen.'

'I haven't got the pen,' said Peter, and wondered how many times during the past forty-eight hours he had made the same remark.

'But you know what it contained

— you found the paper in the cap?' insisted the man in the mask.

'Supposing I did,' snapped Peter angrily. 'What about it?'

The eyes regarding him through the silken slits glittered evilly.

'This about it,' said the voice threateningly, and the tall figure moved forward until the muzzle of the automatic was barely three inches from Peter's stomach. 'If you know what that pen contained you will tell — now — unless you want to go the same way as — the policeman.'

The gloved forefinger moved, compressing slightly on the trigger, and Peter thought rapidly.

'You daren't shoot,' he said, keeping his voice steady with a supreme effort. 'Not in your own interests — for if you kill me I certainly shan't be able to tell you anything about the pen.'

There was a tense silence during which Peter felt the perspiration trickle down his forehead, and then the masked man took a step backwards.

'There is something in what you say,' he muttered, and then, before Peter could fully appreciate the relief that came to him: 'I will try other methods, perhaps less pleasant.'

Without removing his gaze from Peter, he whistled — a soft, low whistle. There was a moment's pause and then the door, which he had closed, opened and a small man came in.

'Biker,' said the man in black, 'you have the chloroform — '

He left the sentence unfinished, nodding his head towards Peter. The little wizened man shot a quick glance round, and took from his pocket a bottle and a pad.

Peter clenched his fists.

'Look here — ' he began angrily, but the masked man stopped him with a peremptory gesture.

'You keep quiet,' he snarled, 'otherwise this gun may go off with unpleasant consequences. Now, Biker.'

Biker advanced with a hideous grin distorting his ugly pock-marked face, and as he came he uncorked the bottle and soaked the pad of cotton wool he held with its contents. Peter smelt the sickly odour, like rotten apples, and the scent made him throw caution to the winds.

'You dirty little rat!' he cried. 'You can keep that stuff away from me!'

He sprang forward and launched himself at the cowering Biker. The man collapsed under Peter's onslaught, and they fell to the floor a struggling mass, with Peter uppermost. The masked man gave an exclamation of anger and stepped forward. Gripping his pistol by the barrel, he raised it, and waiting his opportunity brought it down with his force on the back of Peter's skull. Peter gave a little coughing grunt and rolled over at his feet, unconscious.

★　★　★

Lola Marsh sat on the settee in the tiny consulting room and watched the minute hand of her wrist-watch moving slowly round. Over and over again she blamed herself for having let Peter go, and as the time went on she found it increasingly difficult to master her growing fear.

A hundred visions of what might be

happening at that dark and deserted house, to which he had gone so light-heartedly, flickered before her imagination, and more than once she rose with the intention of going there herself, and finding out what was actually occurring. The goggled man might have gone back after his unsuccessful attempt to capture her. The goggled man — the killer of Harvey Slade — Mr. K. —

Her fear grew until it was a monster choking her. If only she had somebody there with her to whom she could talk! She looked at the telephone with some vague idea of ringing her brother up, but he would be in bed and asleep. Apart from which he had no idea that she had started on her mad visit to the old house — was under the impression that she had gone to bed.

She got up and began walking the room restlessly. Had Peter been successful? Had he found the hidden safe, and would she experience on his return the relief of knowing that those papers were no longer a source of danger?

For some reason or other she felt a

vague foreboding — a subconscious warning of impending peril. It made her start at every sound — the creaking of a floor board; the breeze brushing a branch across the window; the hundred and one night noises that in the country seem to spring up like uneasy ghosts in the darkness.

She ought never to have let him go. She knew the danger more than he — knew the stake for which these people were playing — knew just how desperate they were. If anything happened to Peter, she would feel like a murderess.

She stopped suddenly in her mechanical pacing to and fro — and stood rigid. Was that the click of the gate? She listened.

Yes, she could hear footsteps coming up the gravel path leading to the front door. A wave of relief passed over her as she realized that her fears had been groundless. Here was Peter, and whether he had been successful or not she didn't care. He was back, and that was all that mattered.

She heard the key in the lock and the

door open, and, unable to curb her impatience, went into the little hall.

'I'm so glad,' she began, and stopped, the words frozen on her lips.

Instead of Peter, she could see in the dim shadows the figures of two men, and they were carrying the limp body of a third between them! She heard a snarling oath as the taller of the two dropped his burden and sprang at her, caught a momentary glimpse of a masked face close to her own, and then everything was gone — wiped out by unconsciousness!

12

The Ordeal

Peter Lake slid back to consciousness slowly and to the accompaniment of an ever increasing pain in his head. To ease this he tried to put up his hand to his throbbing temples and found that he could not. He found also that he could not move any of his other limbs either, and opened his eyes.

At first he could see nothing for the light made his head swim; but gradually this passed off and to his astonishment he saw that he was lying on the settee in his own consulting room. How had he got there? And why couldn't he use his arms and legs?

And then he heard the dim murmur of voices, and, raising his head, he saw that besides himself there were two other people in the room — a tall gaunt man whose face was hidden behind a square of black silk, and a little wizened pock-marked fellow. Memory came flooding back, and as it did so he saw the fourth occupant of the room, and a cry escaped his lips.

Bound to a chair so securely that she could not move hand or foot, and with a gag tied round her mouth, was Lola Marsh. Her wide violet-blue eyes were fixed on his with an expression in which fear and relief were curiously mingled.

At his cry the tall man who had been talking to his companion in low tones swung round and corning over to the settee, stood looking down at him.

'Got your senses back have you?' he said, nodding. 'Well, that's good. Now we can talk!'

'Don't talk too much, guv'nor,' interrupted Biker anxiously. 'We 'aven't got all the time in the world.'

'You mind your own business!' snarled Paul Andronsky. 'I'm looking after this job.'

Biker shrugged his narrow shoulders.

'All right,' he protested. 'I'm only tellin' yer that the night doesn't last for ever, and we want ter get done and away before it gets light.'

'We'll do that — you needn't worry,' retorted the masked man. 'Now, Dr. Lake, I hope you are going to be sensible, and save me all further trouble and yourself a great deal of — shall we say inconvenience?'

Peter looked up at him, and his lips compressed.

'I don't know what you're talking about,' he said, weakly, 'but I warn you that you'd better release that girl at once, or — '

'Or what?' broke in Andronsky with a sneer. 'Believe me your threats do not frighten me in the least. I need hardly remind you that you are not in a position to dictate to me. Indeed, the shoe is on the other foot. However, the release of Miss Marsh is entirely in your hands. If you are sensible she will not be harmed in any way.'

'What do you want?' asked Peter, knowing full well but trying to gain time while he forced his brain to cope with the situation.

'I want the green pen which that fool, Ledder, dropped in the drive at 'Five Trees' and which you picked up,' said the masked man. 'Or, alternatively, I want to know what was in it.'

'I haven't got the pen,' said Peter, 'and neither do I know what was in it.'

The eyes behind the black silk regarded him suspiciously.

'Did you give the pen to Ledder then?' asked Andronsky.

'I did not,' replied Peter, 'for the simple reason that it wasn't in my possession.'

'I don't believe you!' snarled the masked man. 'If you didn't give it to Ledder, it's still in your possession.'

'You are at liberty to search the whole house,' retorted Peter, 'and if you can find it you're cleverer than I am.'

Paul Andronsky laughed and shook his head.

'I daresay, my friend,' he answered softly, 'but you are not getting me to waste my time like that. I should prefer you to tell me exactly where that pen is.'

'I'm not good at performing miracles,' said Peter, 'and it would be a miracle if I could tell you where the pen is.'

Andronsky leaned down over the settee until Peter could feel his hot breath fanning his cheek.

'So you insist on sticking to that story do you?' he grated harshly. 'You think you can fool me and get away with it? I warn you, my friend, that you had better change your mind.'

'Look here!' said Peter, staring up at the other steadily. 'Suppose we cut out all this melodramatic rubbish! Once and for all I haven't got the pen! I don't know where it is and I don't know what is in it! Have you got that clear?'

'You put up a very good bluff, Dr. Lake,' said Andronsky, 'and it might have the effect of fooling some people, but it doesn't go with me. I have no wish to resort to strong methods, but unless you are willing to be sensible, I'm afraid I shall have to. For the last time, will you tell me what you have done with that pen?'

'I've said all I've got to say,' snapped Peter angrily, 'and I'm not going to keep up this cross talk any longer!'

Paul Andronsky straightened up to his full height.

'I'm afraid you are labouring under a delusion,' he said, and his voice was vibrant with suppressed anger. 'You will say a great deal more before I've finished with you, and the young lady!'

He turned as he spoke the last words and looked at the girl.

For the first time, Peter felt a twinge of alarm.

'You can leave Miss Marsh out of it,' he said hastily. 'She's got nothing to do with it!'

The man in the mask gave a low malignant chuckle.

'That is another delusion of yours, Dr. Lake,' he sneered. 'You seem to be full of them. Miss Marsh has everything to do with it — as you will see in a few seconds.'

'What do you mean?' demanded Peter.

'If you continue in your pig-headed refusal to divulge what you have done with the pen,' said Paul Andronsky, and there was cold ferocity in his emotionless voice, 'I shall have to take steps to make you! That is where Miss Marsh will be of the greatest assistance.'

The blood receded from Peter's face, leaving it white and strained. There was no mistaking the threat that lay behind the man's words.

Andronsky saw by his expression that he understood his meaning, and laughed again — a hard sound without any vestige of mirth.

'I see that you understand,' he said softly. 'Perhaps, without going to — er — such lengths, you will do what I ask?'

The momentary feeling of cold fear left Peter and was replaced by a flaming anger against this sneering chuckling devil, who was suggesting unnameable things.

'You infernal scoundrel!' he roared, wrenching furiously at the cords which bound his wrists. 'If you touch a hair of that girl's head I'll — '

'You'll do what?' broke in Andronsky harshly. 'What will you do, Dr. Lake? Please tell me. It would interest me.' And then suddenly changing his tone: 'You fool! What can you do? Why not stop all these cheap heroics and be sensible!'

'I've already told you,' panted Peter, 'that even if my life depended on it I couldn't tell you what you want to know!'

'And I have said that I don't believe you,' snarled the masked man. 'Apart from which it is not your life that is in any danger.'

He stopped and turning, looked at the terrified girl.

'Have you noticed,' he went on, 'what really beautiful hands Miss Marsh has? So white and well kept, and with such long tapering fingers. What a pity it would be if anything should happen to spoil them!'

He paused and, with Peter's eyes riveted on him, walked over to a small glass-fronted cabinet in the corner.

'Your profession will save me a great deal of trouble, Dr. Lake,' he murmured, tapping the glass door with a gloved finger. 'Everything I require is here to my hand.'

Peter watched frozen with horror. He knew only too well what that cabinet contained — the rows of shining, razor-sharp surgical instruments that he so conscientiously kept clean, but up to now had had no occasion to use.

'With one of these slender knives,' said Andronsky, 'it will be child's play to remove the fingers from Miss Marsh's beautiful right hand — one by one — '

'You fiend!' burst out Peter through lips that were white and bloodless. 'You can't do it!'

Paul Andronsky shrugged his shoulders, and pulling open the cabinet selected a scalpel which he balanced in one hand.

'I can — and I will — do just that,' he said, 'unless you do what I ask. I am not a skilled surgeon, and I don't expect to perform the — er — operation as well as you would, for instance. There will, no doubt, be considerable pain, and loss of blood — '

'By heaven!' shouted Peter, 'If I was only free — '

'If the earth was made of bread and cheese,' scoffed Andronsky. 'You are making a great fuss, Dr. Lake — a foolish fuss, for what I propose doing is in your power to prevent!'

Peter suppressed a groan. That was just

it, it was not in his power to prevent this outrage, but the fiend in the mask would never believe it.

'Stop!' he cried hoarsely, as Andronsky went over to the girl with the knife in his hand. 'Stop! Listen to me! Don't you realize that I would give up a thousand green pens to stop Miss Marsh from being harmed?'

'I only ask you to give up one,' interrupted the masked man. 'Give me that or tell where it is and I'll go at once.'

'But I can't,' said Peter desperately. 'I keep telling you I can't! Don't you understand plain English?'

'Then I'm afraid we shall have to continue the comedy,' snapped Andronsky. 'I can't afford to waste any further time.' He bent over the white-faced girl and picked up her slender right hand. She shrank away and Peter heard, in spite of the gag, her strangled cry of terror.

'For the love of heaven don't do it,' cried Peter, half-crazy at his helplessness.

Andronsky took no notice, and the glittering knife touched the girl's first finger.

'I hate spoiling anything so beautiful,' he said softly. But you leave me no alternative.'

The keen blade pressed against the soft flesh, and a little line of crimson showed up with startling clearness. Lola Marsh gave a choking cry, and then Bilter, who had been a fascinated and silent spectator hitherto, sprang forward and caught her as she swayed.

'Stop!' cried Peter, the perspiration standing out in great beads on his forehead. 'Stop, I'll tell you what you want to know.'

Andronsky straightened up and his eyes glittered.

'I thought you would,' he said, with a note of triumph in his voice. 'Come, quickly! Tell me where it is?'

Peter collected his scattered wits and lied.

'You'll find the pen in my bedroom,' he said. 'In the chimney. I put it — '

He broke off with a gasp of astonishment as a strange high-pitched voice said:

'Thank you, Dr. Lake! That information is going to be very useful!'

Andronsky gave a hoarse cry and dropped the knife, staring beyond Peter's head at something on the other side of the room.

With an effort Peter twisted round and saw, framed in the open doorway, his head encased in a leather helmet, and the upper part of his face concealed by a pair of mica goggles, the sinister figure of Mr. K.!

13

The End of Andronsky

Chief Inspector William Flower flung the black stub of a cigar into the fireplace, shifted his huge bulk until he was more comfortably settled in the big armchair, carefully arranged a cushion behind his head and sighed. The accommodation which he had secured at the only inn that Higher Wicklow boasted was extremely comfortable.

With his large body at rest in one chair and his feet supported on a second chair, Sweet William pondered on the whole tricky problem.

A telephone message, following his substantial dinner, had given him all the information he wanted to know regarding Ledder. The man had never come in direct contact with the police, neither was he known in 'Records', but he had apparently been the associate and friend of people less fortunate in this respect than himself.

Paul Andronsky, with whom he had been seen on several occasions, was a well-known crook who had served two sentences for fraud, from the last of which he had only just been released. This information gave Mr. Flower food for much thought, for he remembered that the first person to suffer from the elusive Mr. K.'s attentions had been Lew Andronsky, the brother of this recently released convict.

He lit another long, black, evil-smelling cigar and smoked with closed eyes. Yes, undoubtedly, the case was tricky. There were so many people in it.

Mr. Flower opened his eyes, blew a large cloud of rank smoke from his lips, watched it disperse, and closed his eyes again. The girl. He had learned quite a lot about her from the servants, and there was still quite a lot that he wanted to know. For one thing, he was still very anxious to know where she was to be found. Neither the old man nor the old woman could tell him where she lived.

Yes, there was quite a lot of mystery surrounding the girl that wanted clearing up.

Mr. Flower relapsed into such a state of intense mental concentration that anybody seeing him at that moment would have been convinced that he had fallen asleep.

The whole secret lay in that pen — and Mr. K., he finally decided.

The cone of ash on his cigar grew longer and longer and presently dropped on to his waistcoat. But he might have been dead for all the notice he took, and it was not until the glowing end had reached his fingers that he started to wakefulness, and then he became surprisingly wakeful indeed.

The inn had long since closed and the inmates were in bed and asleep — even Mr. Flower himself was a little surprised when he saw the time — but it did not prevent him from putting his suddenly conceived plan into execution.

It has been said by his confreres at Scotland Yard that Chief Inspector William Flower was never known to be fully awake. This gross slander would have been refuted if any of them could have seen him during the following half hour, for in spite of the lateness of the hour, he swiftly donned hat and coat and, creeping down the stairs, let himself silently out into the cold darkness of the night. A sharp glance he gave to right and left, and then set off briskly along the deserted road . . .

★ ★ ★

'So you weren't wise enough to take my advice, Andronsky, eh?' said the high-pitched voice. 'I told you to keep out of this!'

'I don't take orders from anybody!' Paul Andronsky crouched back against the wall glaring hate at the newcomer through the slits in his mask.

'The time is coming very shortly when you won't be *able* to take orders from anybody — except the devil,' answered Mr. K. gently and waved the automatic which he held in his hand. 'In the meanwhile I'm afraid I shall have to take steps to ensure that you do not make a nuisance of yourself.' He turned his head towards the shivering and terrified Bilter, and the light glinting on the mica eye-pieces of his goggles gave him a peculiarly eerie inhuman appearance.

'You there,' he said harshly, 'pull down that curtain from the window, tear it in strips, and tie up our friend here.'

He nodded towards Andronsky. Bilter hesitated, torn between his fear of Andronsky and his terror of Mr. K.

'Come on,' grated the latter sharply. 'Do as you're told, otherwise I shall regret being so lenient.' The muzzle of the automatic moved menacingly and with a little gasp of abject terror Bilter hastened to obey.

Mr. K. watched him in silence.

'That's better,' he said when Andronsky's wrists and ankles had been securely bound and he had examined the knots. 'Now come here.'

Bilter approached, licking his dry lips apprehensively.

'Give me the rest of that curtain stuff,' said the goggled man. 'Now turn round and cross your wrists behind your back.'

Bilter did as he was told, and in a few seconds had been trussed up as securely as his companion.

Mr. K pocketed his pistol and stood surveying his handiwork with satisfaction.

'That's much better,' he remarked.

'What are you going to do with us?' snarled Andronsky, and there was a slight shake in his voice that was not due to anger.

'At the present moment you're all right as you are,' replied Mr. K. 'What I may do with you later I haven't yet decided.' He looked at Peter. 'I am going to collect that pen first. You say it's in the chimney in your bedroom, Dr. Lake? If you will excuse me, I will go and get it.'

He turned abruptly before Peter could reply and went out into the darkness of the hall. A silence followed his exit. What, thought Peter, was going to happen when he discovered that there was no pen in the chimney?

He looked at Andronsky. The masked man was struggling with the bonds at his wrists, and breathing heavily as a result of his exertions. The girl was still slumped in the chair unconscious, a thin trickle of blood running down her fingers. Bilter lay motionless on the floor, his little beady eyes staring at the open door. Peter heard Mr. K. ascending the stairs and presently moving about the room overhead.

An eternity seemed to pass. A whole lifetime crowded into the space of a minute. There was no sound from upstairs, and Peter guessed that Mr. K. was searching in the chimney for the pen that wasn't there.

A sound from the direction of Andronsky made him look over quickly, and with a start of surprise he saw that the masked man had succeeded in freeing his hands. Either Bilter had made a bad job of the tying or the curtain strips had stretched.

Andronsky bent down and tore at the knots at his ankles, a moment later he was free. With a quick glance upwards he went over to the prostrate Bilter and began tugging at the bindings round his wrists. Peter felt his breath coming a little faster. The approach of the crisis was at hand, and what the climax would be it was impossible to guess. Mr. K. would be returning shortly from his useless quest, and then — what would happen?

The sound of footsteps from above became audible once more. They were crossing the floor, quickly, hastily. Mr. K. had examined the chimney and found — nothing. Now he was coming to demand an explanation.

Andronsky heard the steps and stopped in his endeavours to free his companion. With a quick spring, he was across the room and, stooping, picked up the knife which had fallen from his hand at the appearance of the goggled man. Grasping it like a dagger, he tip-toed over to the open doorway, and stood pressed up against the wall at the side of the door.

The footsteps of Mr. K. began to descend the stairs, and Peter saw Andronsky grow rigid.

A dim figure loomed in the doorway, and he opened his mouth to cry out. But even as the cry left his lips Andronsky sprang forward and struck with all his force at the breast of the man crossing the threshold. There was a metallic snap and a snarled oath, and then Andronsky staggered back, glaring at the broken knife in his hand.

'You fool!' snarled Mr. K. 'Do you think you could get me like that? I'm wearing a bullet proof waistcoat.'

He whipped out his automatic from his pocket, and sent three shots tearing through the body of the crouching man before him. Andronsky gave a choking cough, clawed at the air, and pitched forward on his face.

14

Fire!

Taking no notice of Peter's horrified exclamation, Mr. K. walked over to the sprawling body of his victim and spurned it contemptuously with his foot. When he had made quite certain that Andronsky was dead he pocketed the still-smoking automatic and came over to the settee.

'Dr. Lake,' he said calmly as though nothing had happened, 'there is no pen in the chimney. Will you kindly give me an explanation?'

With an effort Peter dragged his eyes away from that huddled body and the ever-widening pool that was spreading over the shabby carpet, and looked up at the goggled man.

'I lied to Andronsky,' he said. 'He wouldn't believe me when I said I hadn't got the pen and didn't know where it was, and so I lied — to stop him torturing Miss Marsh.'

135

He saw the lips compress, and guessed that Mr. K. was frowning.

'And is it true that you don't know the whereabouts of the pen?' asked Mr. K. after a slight pause.

'Perfectly true,' said Peter. 'If I had I should have told Andronsky before he went to the lengths he did.'

There was a silence. The goggled man appeared to be thinking deeply.

'Extraordinary,' he muttered presently. 'Where the devil can it be? You haven't got it, the girl hasn't got it. Ledder didn't get it, and Andronsky obviously didn't get it. Where can it be?'

'I haven't the least idea,' said Peter, answering his spoken thoughts. 'Somebody must have taken it from me while I lay unconscious in that house.'

'There was nobody to take it,' said Mr. K. 'Only the people I have mentioned knew of its significance.' He broke off suddenly, and Peter saw that he was listening intently.

Peter listened too, but at first he could hear nothing, and then from outside came the sound of footsteps on gravel. They stopped, came on again, and stopped

136

once more — uncertain hesitating foot-steps. Mr. K. went over to the door and stood, his head inclined forward into the darkness of the little hall.

Rat-tat, rat-tat. Somebody was knocking softly at the front door. Peter's heart bounded with sudden hope. There was only one person who would be likely to call at that hour, and that was Mr. Flower. And yet the step had not sounded like his, neither was the knock incisive enough. He heard the goggled man utter a soft curse, and saw him move out into the hall and become lost in the blackness. There was a pause, and then the knocking on the front door was repeated, this time a little louder. There was the click of a lock, and then a voice said:

'Can I see Dr. Lake?'

It was followed by a startled cry and the heavy slam of the front door shutting. Before the wondering Peter had time to conjecture what had happened, Mr. K. came back, dragging with him the stooping figure of an elderly man whose lined face was twisted into an expression of sheer terror.

'Now then, what do you want to see Dr. Lake for?' snarled Mr. K., flinging his captive away from him so that he staggered and fell back against the wall.

With a thrill of intense surprise Peter saw that the newcomer was Harvey Slade's old servant. The man was in the last stages of fear. His eyes bulged from his head and his jaws hung loosely. Peter, who had never met the man to speak to before in his life, wondered what on earth had brought him there.

'Now then, out with it!' snapped Mr. K., catching the terrified old man by the arm and shaking him roughly. 'What did you come to see Dr. Lake for?'

The other made an unintelligible sound in his throat.

'Answer me!' cried Mr. K., shaking him again, and then as the old man opened his mouth, he gave a loud exultant exclamation, and tearing back his coat, snatched from his waistcoat pocket something that glinted greenly in the electric light.

Peter echoed his cry in his astonishment, for the thing he held in his hand

138

was the green fountain pen that had belonged to Harvey Slade!

'How did you get this?' hissed Mr. K.

The old man swallowed hard and crouched farther back against the wall.

'I — I took it from Dr. Lake's pocket after 'e was knocked out up at the 'ouse,' he stammered almost inaudibly. 'I didn't mean no 'arm — '

'So you were there that night, were you?' broke in the goggled man. The other nodded feebly.

'Yes, I came back,' he said. 'I wondered why the guv'nor used to send me and the missus away at times, and I thought I'd come back and find out.

'Just as I got back I saw Dr. Lake having a fight with a big chap in the drive, and I saw 'im pick up that pen. I knew it contained the secret of the guv'nor's safe, but I 'adn't no idea of taking it then. It was only arter I got up to the 'ouse and saw 'e'd been killed and that Dr. Lake 'ad been 'it on the 'ead that I thought p'r'haps if I took it I might be able ter open the safe and get a few pickings.

'Then I saw that Dr. Lake was

recovering and I got scared and cleared off. Afterwards when all the fuss was on and the perlice was 'anging about, I didn't like to say anything about it, but the missus thought I didn't ought ter keep it, and p'r'aps if I brought it back to Dr. Lake and explained 'e'd save me from gettin' inter trouble — ' His voice trailed away incoherently.

'So that was it, was it?' muttered Mr. K. 'Well, you couldn't have chosen a better time so far as I'm concerned, though I doubt whether it will be so from your point of view.'

He unscrewed the cap of the pen and carefully extracted a small roll of paper. Spreading it out, he glanced at it quickly and then put it in his pocket.

'I'll make you a present of this,' he said, tossing the pen on to the settee. 'I've got all I want.'

He seized the old man by the arm and dragged him away from the wall, and then, with a strip of curtain that was left over, securely bound his wrists and ankles.

'Now you're all comfy,' he said with a quick glance round.

'Yer ain't going ter leave me like this,' whined Bilter, 'fer the perlice ter find? Don't do that guv'nor. You've got what you wanted, and I ain't done nothin' ter 'arm yer. Let me go — '

'The police won't find you, I promise that,' said Mr. K. 'There will, in fact, be nothing for them to find.'

His words made Peter go suddenly cold. What further devilry had the man planned? A second later he had discovered and was appalled, for Mr. K. without another word, went swiftly over to the window, tore down the remaining curtain and draped it over Peter's desk. A pile of newspapers on a corner table he fetched over and scattered on top of the curtain, and then, from his pocket, he produced a petrol lighter, snapped it open and applied the flame to the flimsy curtain stuff. It caught at once, and a long yellow tongue of fire engulfed the desk, licking hungrily at the dry woodwork.

Mr. K. turned quickly.

'Goodbye,' he said, and walked to the door. 'The dawn is always a little chilly, but I think you will be warm enough!'

Mr. William Flower plodded along the deserted country road, his mind fully occupied in turning over the idea that had come to him. It was a long way from the inn to 'Five Trees' and Sweet William hated exercise of any sort, but he went on his fat legs covering the ground at a surprising speed.

He reached the dark forbidding entrance to the drive and paused, looking about him for the man on guard. But there was no sign of him. The winding tree-bordered stretch of moss-covered gravel faded into the blackness, empty and devoid of life.

Mr. Flower grunted. The constable, of course, was on his rounds somewhere up by the house. The stout inspector entered the gates and began to walk up the avenue. He came in sight of the house — dark, gloomy and uninviting — and paused again. Still no sign of the constable.

He moved on again towards the house and rounded the angle of the side wall. Here the overshadowing trees formed a patch of dense blackness, and Mr. Flower had to pick his way carefully. He had not gone more than eight yards when his foot caught in something, and he stumbled and nearly fell. The muttered curse which had risen to his lips died as his hand, which he had flung out to save himself, came in contact with — flesh!

He sat back on his haunches and fumbled in his pocket for a box of matches, his heart beating fast. The first match blew out, but the second he shielded with his palm, and in its feeble glimmer he saw the motionless form and white, upturned face of the constable. He was stone dead, and across his mouth still rested the chloroform-soaked pad of cotton-wool that had killed him.

Sweet William grunted, and got to his feet as the match burned to his fingers and went out. He was by no means a coward, but he gave a quick and uneasy glance behind him as he stood in the darkness. Was the murderer of the constable still lurking somewhere near the house? Watching him, perhaps, from the concealment of that sweeping belt of shrubbery.

The hair stirred slightly on his neck, and then he gave himself a shake. This would never do. He was giving way to nerves. A man had been killed in the execution of his duty, and it was his duty to pull in the killer.

Leaving the body where he had found it, he walked round the house, keeping as sharp a lookout as he could. But there was no sight or sound of any other living presence.

He decided to go, and set off down the drive at a run.

He was panting heavily from his unusual exertion as he came up the village High Street, and then at the far end he saw a glow of light — an ominous red glow that cast a ruddy glare on the roadway. Dark figures were moving in the light of the flames, and as he breathlessly rounded the bend of the road and came in sight of the blazing house, the last of his breath left him in a gasp of surprise. The house that was burning so furiously was Dr. Lake's!

* * *

The wind whispered softly high up in the tree-tops round 'Five Trees,' and blew gently in cool, caressing gusts over the white face of the dead man who lay under the shadow of those gloomy walls, staring sightlessly into the black vault of the sky. It blew gently in at the half-open window of the dining room and stirred the curtains as though unseen fingers were pulling them inside, and sent little breaths through the open door into the dark hall, but the closed door of the study checked it.

Behind that closed door, in the big room where Harvey Slade had lived and worked and died, the man who had killed him sent the dancing light of a torch leaping over the dim apartment.

He was breathing quickly with excitement as he advanced to the huge desk that occupied the centre of the room and, standing beside, consulted the slip of paper in his hand. He had pushed his goggles up on to his forehead, and his eyes, as he scanned the written lines, were full of greed. Here, close at hand, was the fortune that old Slade had tried to do him out of. Half of it at least was his by right, for it had been his brain that had put it into Slade's possession. Fifty-fifty had been the arrangement, and he had been content with that. But Slade hadn't. Slade had wanted the lot, and more! Well, he was dead, and now he would get nothing.

He swung the torch round and directed its light on to one of the massive carved legs of the desk. The third acorn — that was it! He felt along the wood and pressed. There was a faint click as a piece of the carving sank beneath his thumb. And that was all — nothing else happened. He scowled and looked at the slip of paper again. Yes, he had followed the directions, but —

He flashed the torch around him and then he saw what he had not noticed before. A small block of the parquet flooring near the desk had risen on end. He went over eagerly and, directing his light into the cavity, saw a small, polished steel knob projecting. Kneeling down, he put in his hand and grasping the knob, he pulled . . .

15

Raining Money

Peter watched the fire rapidly gaining ground with a feeling of helpless despair. So this was the end. In less than an hour, unless somebody came to their rescue, they would be burned up in that holocaust — black, charred, unrecognizable.

Peter racked his brains to find some way out of this death-trap. The desk was blazing furiously, and the carpet near where it stood had started to smoulder. It was this that gave him his idea. With a desperate effort he rolled himself off the settee, falling with a thud that shook the room and sent a shower of sparks flying up from the burning wood. With difficulty he rolled himself over towards the blazing mass where the fire had started, and then, gritting his teeth, he thrust his bound wrist into the flame.

The pain was excruciating, and he had

to bite his tongue to prevent the cry which rose in his throat escaping. The sweat poured down his forehead, but he achieved his object. In a little while he felt his bonds give, and then as he jerked his wrists apart they snapped.

His hands and wrists were scorched and blistered, but he was free. With frantic haste he untied his ankles and staggered to his feet. An instant later he was bending over Lola and feverishly tugging at the knots that bound her.

'You get outside and wait for me,' he said chokingly as the smoke caught at his throat and set him coughing. She hesitated, but he helped her to her feet and pushed her towards the door.

'Go quickly,' he said. 'I'll follow you in a second.'

She obeyed and going over to Biker he stooped and set the little crook free. The strain of the last few seconds had been too much for the man. He had fainted. Peter picked him up, carried him across the hall to the front door and slung him out into the garden. Then he went back for the old servant. By the time he had released him the whole room was blazing furiously, and even as he and the old man reached the door he heard a crash as the ceiling in one corner fell.

Lola Marsh was waiting by the front door, and as they came into the cool air, with eyes smarting and streaming from the effects of the smoke, she grasped his arm.

Blindly she led him down the little path, the old servant stumbling along behind them, through the gate and out into the roadway, which was lit almost to the brightness of day by the lurid, rapidly spreading flames from the burning house.

As Peter paused and wiped his streaming forehead with the back of his hand he heard the irregular thudding of approaching footsteps. Turning he saw a man running jerkily towards them — a big man who was panting heavily — and as he came into the light Peter recognized him.

'Mr. Flower!' he gasped, and the runner stopped.

'What's been happening here?' panted Sweet William with difficulty; and as briefly as he could Peter told him.

'Then he's gone to the house — 'Five Trees',' snapped the stout inspector. 'If we're quick we can catch him — wait there!'

He was off again, leaving Peter standing in the roadway with Lola Marsh, and the terrified servant.

The girl touched him on the arm, and looking down into her upturned face, Peter saw that it was troubled.

'If — if the police catch Mr. K. and open that safe,' she whispered, 'they'll find those papers.'

'I'm afraid they will,' broke in Peter, 'and I don't see how we are going to prevent it. The only thing you can do is tell Flower the truth. He seems a decent sort.'

'He'll never believe my story,' she said, shaking her head. 'But I suppose it's the only thing to do now.'

The fire had at last attracted the attention of the sleeping villagers, and excited voices heralded the appearance of partially dressed members of the community.

They came running towards the spot and surrounded the little group, gesticulating violently, and all speaking at once. Before Peter could answer any of their questions, however, the sound of a motor-horn sent them scattering, and an open Ford drew up beside Peter with a shrill squeaking of brakes.

'Jump in,' called the voice of Sweet William from the back, 'both of you, and bring the old man with you.'

Peter bundled the dazed old man in with Mr. Flower and his companion, whom he recognized as Inspector Bullot. He had barely had time to scramble in himself before the car started with a jerk and shot off up the High Street. Fifty yards away from the drive entrance to 'Five Trees,' the chief inspector stopped it.

'We don't want to let him know we've come,' he said as he got out. 'You come with us, Dr. Lake. Miss Marsh can stop here with Sergeant Dobson.'

Lola opened her lips to protest, thought better of it and remained silent, but Peter caught her appealing glance as he followed Bullot and Sweet William, and gave her a nod of encouragement.

The drive was black and silent as they entered it, and picking their way noiselessly on the grassy border, made towards the house. The dark bulk of the building loomed up evil and sinister against the faint grey that streaked the eastern sky. Suddenly Mr. Flower uttered a hissing warning and Peter felt his arm gripped.

'He's there!' said the stout man and there was a tinge or excitement in his voice and Peter saw a momentary flash from one of the windows.

Cautiously they crept forward.

'If possible,' whispered Mr. Flower, 'we want to take him by surprise.'

But it was he who got the surprise, for the end of his sentence was drowned in a shattering explosion that shook the earth beneath their feet and came echoing back from the surrounding hills. The dark bulk of the house was split by a gigantic sheet of white-hot flame, and before their eyes they saw the walls crumble.

'My God!' cried Peter. 'What's happened?'

Sweet William, without answering, began to run towards the ruin that had been 'Five Trees' and then he stopped, sheltering beneath the trees that lined the drive, for the air suddenly became filled with falling debris. It fell around them thickly, striking the ground with dull thuds and pattering on the leaves above them like rain. Something fluttered into Peter's face, and he grabbed it — an oblong white object that cracked in his fingers. In the darkness he caught sight of other dim white shapes that fluttered round him like falling leaves.

The feel of the thing he held brought an exclamation of amazement to his lips.

'Have you got a light?' he asked hoarsely, and Bullot produced a torch and flashed it on.

Peter gave one glance at the object in his hand in the white beam and turned to Mr. Flower.

'Gosh! Look at this!' he exclaimed. 'And there's more of them — all round us.'

Mr. Flower's large face discarded its habitual half-sleepy, wholly-bored expression.

'Well, I never!' he breathed in astonishment. 'It's raining money!'

Peter was holding a Bank of England note for a hundred pounds!

★　★　★

153

The explosion had destroyed the greater part of the house and with it the man known as Mr. K. Certain portions of a human body were found among the ruins, but so mangled as to defy identification. This was not necessary, as it turned out, for the question as to whom Mr. K. had been was settled, definitely once and for all, when a frightened woman came into the little police station at Higher Wicklow and laid before Inspector Flower certain information.

Mr. Flower later in the afternoon called to see Peter at his temporary lodgings in Higher Wicklow's one and only inn, and Peter listened stunned to the revelation that was made to him.

'George Arlington!' he gasped, stupefied. 'Impossible!'

Sweet William looked at him, sadly.

'Nuthin's impossible,' he murmured gently. 'You'll realize that when you reach my age. And this certainly isn't. George Arlington was Mr. K. all right. His housekeeper got frightened when she found that his bed hadn't been slept in and he was nowhere to be found, and came to us. We found all the information we wanted at his house. Apparently he and Slade had been partners for months in the fencing business. So far as I can make out Arlington did the actual negotiations, and Slade's job was to get rid of the stolen stuff and convert it into cash.

'If any of the people they dealt with wouldn't sell for the price they offered, or offended them in any way, Arlington tipped 'em off to the police by sending one of the 'K' letters. Everythin' would have been all right if Slade, who didn't know that 'Mr. K.' was Arlington, hadn't found out and tried a little blackmailing. I found the letter he wrote among Arlington's effects. He refused to share out the proceeds and threatened to give Arlington away — not to the police, mark you — he couldn't do that without incriminatin' himself — but to the crooks whom Arlington had squealed on. Arlington realized his danger and killed him.'

'But,' protested Peter, 'I was with Arlington the night Slade was killed. So how could he — '

'He could and he did,' broke in Sweet William. 'He killed him after you'd left.' He frowned. 'You walked, didn't you? Well, he rode in that fast car of his and came to 'Five Trees' by the other way. An' he had just killed Slade when Ledder turned up.

'If Arlington had known who it was he would have probably killed him too, but he thought it was the police. You see, Slade expected Arlington that night and expected trouble. He realized that he was playing with fire, and he took the precaution of sending that letter to the Yard — he was an illiterate man — and when Arlington arrived an' started threatenin' he told him he'd sent it. What was in Slade's mind when he sent it I can't rightly say, but I think his idea was to use it as a sort of protection, an' if things went wrong with him — and they did — that the police would arrive quickly enough to pinch the man who had killed him.

'Anyhow, Arlington cleared off, and Ledder, who had expected to find a live man, was shocked to find a dead one; so startled that he only waited long enough to take the pen and clear off.'

'How did he know anything about the pen?' asked Peter.

'Andronsky and he and that feller Bilter had been working to get it for months,' said Mr. Flower. 'They knew Slade kept all his money in the house, and they discovered that the secret was hidden in the pen.' A slow smile broke over his large face. 'Slade had the last laugh, anyhow,' he went on. 'He must have arranged that explosive to guard his treasures and, thinkin' that Arlington might get the better of him, put false instructions in the pen to make sure that nobody 'ud benefit.'

'Well, you seem to know all about it,' said Peter. 'How did you find all this out?'

'Partly from what I found at Arlington's, partly through what Biker has spilt, but mostly by my own brains,' retorted Mr. Flower. 'There's only one thing I can't quite fit in and that's how the girl comes into it. She's not very important, anyway.'

★　★　★

It was three months later when Peter saw Mr. Flower again. He was coming out of Cook's office at Charing Cross and ran into the stout inspector walking slowly along the pavement.

'Hello,' said Mr. Flower and eyeing the tickets in Peter's hand: 'Goin' away?'

Peter nodded.

'I've got a job abroad,' he said. 'By the way, I think you know my wife.'

Mr. Flower looked at the smiling girl who had joined them.

'I think I do,' he replied. 'Married, are you? Well, well, I wish I'd have known, I'd have sent you some flowers on your weddin' day.'

'You're not too late now,' said Peter. 'We were married this morning.'

The Casebooks
of Adam Kane

1

The Able Mr. Kane

The clients' chair, shabby from long usage, but still comfortable, that faced the broad, scrupulously tidy desk, behind which Mr. Adam Kane was sitting, had been occupied by a variety of people during the thirty years of his practice in the legal profession, but the girl who sat there now was something quite out of the ordinary. She was young, twenty-two or twenty-four Mr. Kane thought, and Miss World might have emulated her figure but could certainly not have surpassed it.

Her hair was the colour of a ripe horse-chestnut flecked with little glints of copper where the light from the overhead electric bulb caught it, and it rippled softly down to her shoulders. Her maxi-coat of bottle-green had fallen open as she sat down revealing her long, beautifully-shaped legs in their knee-length, close-fitting boots of soft white leather. Mr. Kane found it very difficult to concentrate his attention away from her legs.

'Why did you insist on half-past nine in the evening, when you phoned this morning to make an appointment?' he asked. 'It's an unusual hour to consult a lawyer.'

'You are an unusual lawyer, Mr. Kane,' she replied smoothly. There was just the trace of huskiness in her low voice. 'You have unusual clients and you often see them at unusual hours, don't you?'

'Sometimes,' said Kane. 'It depends a great deal . . . '

'On what they want and who they are?' she interrupted, quickly. 'You're not very scrupulous, are you? I know a lot about you, Mr. Kane.'

She looked straight at him. Her eyes, under the long, dark lashes, were a deep shade of blue.

'Apparently,' he retorted, helping himself to a cigarette and offering her the box. 'You didn't come here just to tell me that, Miss Nicholls. How can I help you?'

She ignored the box of cigarettes and he lit his own.

'If you were an ordinary solicitor, I shouldn't be here,' she said. 'You've been mixed up in a lot of queer cases . . . '

'Are you trying to get me mixed up in another?' he broke in quickly.

She shook her head, and the copper glints in her hair danced.

'I'm trying to *stop* you getting mixed up in one,' she answered.

Adam Kane raised his eyebrows and let the smoke from his cigarette trickle out through his nostrils.

'Really?' he said. 'That's very interesting. Tell me how?'

She leaned forward a little. Her expression was very earnest.

'You have an appointment with a man named Richard Grennit tomorrow morning,' she said. 'Don't see him. Don't have anything to do with him!'

'Why not?' demanded Kane.

'He's dangerous,' she answered seriously. 'It will mean trouble for you, trouble for a lot of people, trouble for *me*.'

Kane laughed.

'Now we're getting down to the real

reason you don't wish me to see this man,' he said. 'What trouble can Grennit make for you?'

'I'd rather not tell you that . . . ' she began and he cut in swiftly.

'Nothing doing,' he said. 'Do you seriously expect me to turn down a possibly profitable client just because you ask me? You'll have to do better than that, Miss Nicholls — much better.'

For answer she opened the large white suede bag she carried slung from one shoulder, and took out of it a thin packet.

'There's a hundred pounds here,' she said, holding it out to him. 'It's yours — if you agree not to see Grennit.'

Kane's eyes narrowed.

'What makes you think I can be bribed, Miss Nicholls?' he asked. 'Anyhow, Grennit might pay more. How about that?'

She let the packet of money drop onto her lap, uncrossed her legs and re-crossed them.

'Please, do what I ask,' she said, and her husky voice held a faint pleading note. 'If the money isn't enough, perhaps . . . ' She hesitated. 'Perhaps . . . there's something else . . . I could do?'

Not very subtle, thought Kane, but very tempting. I might even get the money as well . . .

'Sorry,' he said, more briskly than he intended. 'If you tell me the truth — why you don't want me to see Grennit — I might reconsider it. Otherwise, nothing doing.'

Her expression changed. The seductive softness drained from her eyes, leaving them very hard. She opened her mouth to speak and Kane had a feeling that what she was going to say would have been crude and very forceful. But she never said it. The buzzer of the telephone stopped her.

Kane grabbed the receiver. The telephone chattered excitedly and he grunted monosyllabic replies. After a minute or two, he put down the receiver and leaned back in his chair. Suddenly he got up, and came round the desk. For a moment he stood looking down at her, thoughtfully. Then he said:

'All right. I'll agree not to have

anything to do with Grennit — for a hundred pounds.'

She looked up at him in surprise. Then she held out the money. Kane took it, riffled through the notes, and put them in his pocket.

'Why did you change your mind?' she asked.

'Because Grennit's dead,' he answered. 'Somebody shot him in his flat a few minutes ago.'

★ ★ ★

Adam Kane stood in the doorway of the living room in Richard Grennit's flat; behind him, her face expressionless, Ann Nicholls peered over his shoulder. The room was a nice room, furnished expensively and with taste. The only discordant note was the stout, balding man who sprawled untidily on the rug in front of the fireplace. There was blood under his head that had oozed down from the bullet wound in his forehead . . .

There were three other men in the room, searching carefully and diligently, systematically and patiently. One of them, a heavily built man with pale, shrewd eyes, came over to Kane.

'Move fast, don't you?' he said. 'What do you know about this?'

'Nothing at all,' answered Kane, staring at the dead man. 'What do you?'

'About the same, at present,' grunted Inspector Cartwright. 'Your name and address was scribbled on his blotting pad — that's why I phoned you . . . '

'He was coming to see me in the morning,' broke in Kane. 'That's all I know about him, Cartwright. Can't help you.'

The Inspector looked unconvinced. He knew Adam Kane of old. He was a first-class lawyer but tricky. He was prepared to take advantage of any loophole the law offered and sometimes he'd make the loopholes, but he was a strict stickler for justice with a capital J and he never tried to prove a client innocent if that client was really guilty.

'I was hoping you were the dead man's lawyer,' he said. Kane shook his head. His restless eyes were darting about the room, coming to rest at last on an object lying on a sheet of newspaper on a small side table.

'Is that the weapon?' he asked.

Cartwright nodded.

'Yes. Two shots were fired. One hit the wall — the other got him in the head. No prints.'

'Which makes it murder, eh?' said Kane. He went over and looked at the gun. 'Hair-trigger. H'm. How did you know about the shooting?'

'The porter,' answered the Inspector. 'And the woman in the next flat. They both heard the shot. She's an invalid and has an arrangement with the porter to call every night at half-past nine to post any letters she may have. He found Grennit like this and called the police . . . '

'Can I go?' called Ann Nicholls from the doorway, 'I feel a bit sick.'

'Who's the bird?' asked Cartwright, under his breath.

'Miss Nicholls. She was in my office when your call came through. She knew Grennit . . . '

'Did she, now?' said the Inspector, with

interest. 'Well, well . . . '

'I can't help you,' Ann broke in. 'I didn't know him very well . . . '

'Tell him why you were so anxious I shouldn't keep my appointment with Grennit,' said Kane, and she frowned.

'You didn't have to . . . ' she began and Cartwright interrupted.

'What's that?' he snapped. 'Why didn't you want Mr. Kane to keep his appointment with the dead man, eh? Why didn't you?'

She looked at Kane.

'Go on,' he said, 'Tell him.'

'I — I've been paying him money — a lot of money — for a long time. I couldn't go on paying . . . He threatened to go to Mr. Kane . . . '

'Blackmail, eh?' said Cartwright. 'What was the hold he had over you?'

'I'm engaged to Viscount Boxmoor . . . Before I met him I lived with — with someone for nearly two years. Grennit got hold of some letters I'd written to this man . . . He threatened to send them to Viscount Boxmoor's family if . . . '

'If you didn't pay up, eh?' grunted the

Inspector. 'Thought that sort of thing was old hat in this permissive age . . . '

'Boxmoor's a relic of the Victorians,' said Kane. 'His family are even worse than he is — stiff-necked and chock-full of morality — puritan breed . . . What's all this wet on the rug?'

'Water, I think,' answered Cartwright impatiently. He looked at Ann Nicholls suspiciously. 'Blackmail's a pretty good motive for murder . . . '

'I was with Mr. Kane in his office when you rang up,' she broke in quickly.

'He might have been doing the same thing to someone else,' said the Inspector. 'What's that you've got, Kane?'

'A rubber band,' answered Kane, snapping it between his fingers.

'There's a whole boxful over here,' put in the man who was searching the desk. 'Some of 'em have spilled on the floor.'

Cartwright shrugged his broad shoulders.

'Thought you'd found something important, eh?' he said.

'It seems pretty obvious to me,' Kane remarked. 'Have you questioned the porter? Anyone called to see Grennit this evening?'

'No,' said Cartwright. 'The porter sits in a kind of glass cubby-hole in the entrance. He'd have seen if anyone had come.'

'I'll bet there's a fire escape, isn't there?'

'Iron stairway at the back,' replied the Inspector. 'Think the murderer came that way?'

'No,' said Kane. 'It's plain enough. A neat set-up.'

'If you know anything, let's hear it,' grunted Cartwright. 'What do you mean by a 'neat set-up'?'

Adam Kane took a cigarette from his case, thought better of it and put it back again. He looked across at Ann Nicholls.

'You tell him,' he said.

'I don't know what you're talking about,' she said.

'All right,' said Kane. 'I'll tell *you*. If Grennit was blackmailing you and you couldn't pay why should he make an appointment with me? He wouldn't. He'd have contacted Boxmoor and his family as he threatened. But if it was the other way round that's exactly what he would have done.'

'I still don't know . . . ' began Ann

Nicholls but he cut her short.

'Grennit refused to pay up any longer, didn't he?' continued Adam Kane. 'He told you he was going to consult me and you got in a panic. But you didn't come to my office to buy me off. You knew that Grennit wouldn't be able to keep that appointment. You came because you wanted to use me as an alibi . . . '

'You must be mad!' exclaimed Ann Nicholls angrily.

'Your little mind has been working overtime, my dear,' went on Kane, ignoring the interruption. 'When you'd decided to kill Grennit, you made an appointment to see me in my office at nine-thirty tonight. You come here about a quarter to nine, slip in when the porter isn't looking, shoot Grennit, and hop away down the fire escape. You knew all about the porter calling on the invalid lady at half-past nine every night — Grennit had probably mentioned it some time or other. You drive to my office, arriving at half-past nine, and give me all that waffle so that I can prove that you were with me at the time Grennit is supposed to have been killed . . . '

'Supposed?' broke in Cartwright, puzzled.

'She shot Grennit earlier, using a silencer. That gun's got a hair-trigger. She takes off the silencer and slips that rubber band through the trigger-guard, round the trigger, and takes both ends of the rubber band and loops them round the butt. The pull will be sufficient to fire a hair-trigger. But she prevents it pulling by wedging a piece of ice from the fridge between the trigger *and the trigger-guard*. When the ice melts, the gun goes off. The bullet lodges in the wall — it might have gone anywhere. *That* was the shot that the porter heard. The shock, of course, jerked off the rubber band . . . '

'It's lies, all lies,' cried Ann Nicholls. 'I tell you it's . . . '

'Tell it to the jury,' snapped Adam Kane. He moved forward swiftly and grabbed the suede handbag hanging from her shoulder. With a quick twist he shot the entire contents out on the floor.

'One perfectly good silencer,' he said. He sniffed at the barrel. 'Recently used, too. You've still got two tiny spots of blood on one of those extremely attractive white boots. You can't afford to overlook these details . . . '

Ann Nicholls, her face no longer beautiful, made a quick dart for the gun on the side table, but Cartwright was too alert. He gripped her arm and swung her round.

'You'll have to come to the station and make a statement,' he said. 'That silencer's going to take a lot of explaining . . . '

She said nothing until she was being led out the door. Then she turned and looked at Kane with concentrated hatred in her eyes.

'You bloody bastard!' she said between her clenched teeth.

Adam Kane, who was lighting a cigarette, smiled pleasantly.

'I thought that was a secret known only to my parents,' he said.

2

The Will and the Way

The numerous clients who came to Adam Kane's offices to consult that astute and unorthodox solicitor were invariably surprised when they met his secretary, for they expected something more glamorous and sexy than the definitely drab and unexciting Anna Kesson. Mr. Kane had a reputation concerning women that quite naturally led to this expectation, and the reality was disappointing. Anna Kesson was dumpy, grey-haired, and slightly masculine, but Mr. Kane found her an invaluable asset because as well as being an example of effortless efficiency, she was the possessor of a remarkable memory. She never forgot anything she had once seen, read, or been told, and was able at a moment's notice to extract any desired item of information from her mental filing-cabinet and repeat it with perfect accuracy, as though her brain was a tape-recorder. It was this rare ability on the part of his secretary that enabled Mr. Kane to spot the salient point in the matter of Alec Henderson and his father's will, although the item contributed by Anna Kesson had nothing to do with the case at all.

Alec Henderson was a youngish man, somewhere in his late twenties, with a round face, slightly surprised eyes, and red hair of the least pleasant of all the shades in that category.

'I was advised to consult you,' he said, sitting down in the comfortable chair facing Mr. Kane across the broad, neat desk, 'because I'm told you specialise in unusual legal problems. Mine is certainly unusual, probably impossible.'

'That's a good start,' said Kane. 'Let's hear it.'

'It concerns my late father's will,' said Alec Henderson. 'It disinherits me entirely. I want to know if it can be contested.'

'Have you brought a copy of the will?'

'Yes.'

From his breast pocket, Henderson

took out a long envelope which he passed across the desk to Mr. Kane. The solicitor extracted a thin document bound with green tape and spread it out in front of him.

Long practice enabled him to read very quickly and accurately and the will was quite short.

'This appears to be in order,' he said, when he had finished. 'Properly attested, signed, and witnessed . . . '

'It ought to be,' broke in Henderson. 'It was drawn up by my father's solicitor, Mr. Benyon. But it's all wrong — I *know* it's all wrong.'

'Why?'

'It's not like my father. He would never have disinherited me. We were always on the best of terms.'

'The beneficiary under this will is a Mrs. Isobel Maitland. Who is she?'

'I don't know. You see what I mean? I'd never heard of this woman before. My father never mentioned her. Why should he suddenly take it into his head to leave her everything?'

'Not very difficult to think of a reason,

is it? Your father was a widower?'

'I know what you're suggesting but he wasn't like that.'

'Don't be naive,' said Mr. Kane, lighting a cigarette. 'I acted for a bishop once. Nobody thought *he* was like that. But he was. Have you seen this woman?'

'Once. In Benyon's office when he read the will.'

'What's she like? Young, attractive, sexy?'

'Not a bit like that. About forty-five, stoutish, not the least sexy.'

Adam Kane drew in the smoke from his cigarette and let it trickle gently from his thin nostrils.

'The will,' he said, after a little pause, 'is dated seventeen days ago. Do you know in what circumstances it was executed?'

'There's no secret about that,' answered Henderson. 'My father had been ill for some time, bad heart trouble, and the doctor insisted on his staying in bed. Three days before his death he sent for Benyon and instructed him to draw up that will . . .'

'The will was signed and witnessed in Mr. Benyon's presence?

'That's right.'

Mr. Kane's lips formed themselves into a small circle, but the whistle remained silent.

'On the face of it, I'd say that an egg under a ten ton steam-hammer 'ud stand more chance of staying intact than you have of successfully contesting this will,' he said.

'Does that mean you're not going to have a try? I thought you liked tackling forlorn hopes.'

'I've not said I'm giving it up. Wait until I do.' Mr. Kane neatly deposited a cylinder of ash from his cigarette in the cut-glass tray on the desk beside him. 'Where were you when all this happened?'

'Up in Scotland, doing my job,' answered Henderson. 'I'm representative for a firm of manufacturing chemists, Hookfield and Paget. I didn't know about my father's illness or his death until I got back. I have to travel about from town to town, you see. Nobody could get in touch with me.'

Mr. Kane's thin, dark brows drew down over his eyes. With his lean face and black hair, Henderson thought he looked positively satanic. It was Kane's normal expression when he was concentrating.

'This wants thinking about,' he said, breaking the short silence. 'It's difficult, probably not possible. You'd better come back on Friday morning. That'll give me three days to consider whether anything can be done or not. Make the appointment with my secretary as you go out.'

When Alec Henderson had gone, Mr. Kane stubbed out his cigarette in the ashtray, lit another, and reread the will. Then he leaned back in his padded chair and stared through the layers of tobacco smoke at the ceiling.

The will appeared to be quite genuine. A person was entitled to leave his possessions to whom he pleased — in certain conditions. He must know what he was doing and he must not be coerced in any way — the subject of undue influence. Had Thomas Henderson been of sufficiently sound mind to know what he was doing when he made his will? Alternatively, had undue influence been brought to bear, such as blackmail, on the freedom of his choice? If either of these could be proved, then the will might be contested.

Mr. Kane flipped down the switch of the intercom communicating with his secretary's office.

'Make an appointment for me to see Mr. Benyon, of Benyon, Gunter and Benyon, Bedford Row,' he said. 'This afternoon, if possible.'

When, a few minutes later, she called back to tell him she'd made an appointment for three-forty-five, Mr. Kane went out to lunch.

Adam Kane lunched at his favourite restaurant, lingering over the meal in thoughtful contemplation, and smoking two cigarettes with his coffee and brandy. At three-forty-five precisely a taxi deposited him at the offices of Benyon, Gunter and Benyon and a few seconds later he was shown into Mr. Benyon's private office.

Mr. Benyon, the only surviving member of the firm, was a thin, unhappy-looking man in his early sixties, with nervous hands on which the tight skin looked dry and powdery.

'I understand,' he said, in a voice that

matched his hands, 'that you have been consulted by Alec Henderson with regard to the will of the late Thomas Henderson?'

'Yes,' answered Mr. Kane. 'What's your opinion of it?'

Mr. Benyon raised what remained of his eyebrows in faint surprise.

'The will is legally sound . . . '

'Doesn't it seem odd to you that Henderson should leave everything to this woman, Maitland?' broke in Kane. 'What do you know about her?'

'Really nothing very much,' said Mr. Benyon.

'Was he in a sufficiently sound mental state to know what he was doing?'

'Certainly!' Mr. Benyon looked a little shocked. 'I should not have executed the will otherwise.'

'Did you read it to him?'

'I read it to him.'

'How long have you been acting as legal adviser to the late Thomas Henderson?'

'For well over thirty years. I cannot quite see . . . '

'You took no steps to prevent this unjust will?'

'It was my duty to take my client's instructions,' said Mr. Benyon, with dignity. 'I pointed out how unfair the will was in completely disinheriting his son, but he was adamant.'

'Didn't Henderson make any explanation about the woman?'

'Only that she was a lady he had known in his younger days.'

'A wild cat, eh? You'd never heard of her before, though, is that right?'

'Quite right . . . '

'Didn't it strike you that she might be using some kind of undue influence over him? Blackmail, perhaps?'

'No, sir, it did not!' declared Mr. Benyon, angrily. 'There was nothing about my late client at the time to suggest that he was acting under duress.'

Mr. Kane ignored this momentary outburst.

'How much money is involved?' he asked.

'Approximately one hundred and forty thousand pounds,' answered Mr. Benyon, more calmly. 'Shares to the value of one hundred and twenty thousand and the house, 'North-gates', which is worth at least thirty thousand.'

'Quite a nice little sum to play about with,' said Adam Kane. 'I presume these shares are deposited with the bank?'

Mr. Benyon inclined his head.

'The bank is appointed executor of the will,' he said. 'It's all very straight-forward . . . '

'You may be right,' said Mr. Kane, pleasantly. 'We shall see.'

Shortly after half-past ten on the following morning, Mr. Kane stood on the front doorstep of a small, semi-detached house in Surbiton and awaited an answer to his ring. When, after an appreciable interval, the door was opened by a woman in a pink overall, he decided that if this was Mrs. Isobel Maintree she was not in the least attractive or sexy. She was short and lumpy with a slightly puffy face, faintly mauve in colour, and covered with tiny red veins, and her eyes were small and pig-like. Her hair was a dull brown, quite lifeless.

'Mrs. Maintree?' Kane inquired.

'Yes, what do you want?' The voice was thick and a trifle common. Mr. Kane explained who he was.

'I am acting for my client, Mr. Alec Henderson,' he continued. 'There are one or two matters I'd like to discuss with you, if you can spare the time.' Mr. Kane could be very polite when it suited him. Mrs. Isobel Maintree opened the door wider.

'You'd better come in,' she said, standing aside to let him pass her. 'You'll have to excuse the mess. I haven't got around to cleaning up this mornin'.'

Or for many mornings, thought Mr. Kane, as she ushered him into a very untidy and dusty sitting room. There were several dirty cups and saucers, plates, and glasses on the centre table, and some stockings hung over the back of a chair. His sharp eyes saw a nearly empty bottle of gin among the litter on the sideboard and the reason for Mrs. Maintree's complexion and puffiness was plain.

'Sit down, won't you?' she said, pushing forward a chair. 'What is it you want to know?'

'It's really a question of curiosity more than anything else,' said Mr. Kane, sitting down and turning on all the considerable charm he could exert when he wished. 'My client is interested to know how you came to meet his father and how long you knew each other?'

'I'd rather not talk about it,' she said, shortly.

'I assure you I have no wish to pry into your private affairs,' said Mr. Kane, who could lie with the greatest conviction, 'but my client had always been led to believe that he was to be the sole beneficiary on the death of his father . . . '

'A man's at liberty to do what he likes with his own, isn't he?' she broke in.

'Certainly,' agreed Mr. Kane, smoothly. 'There is no question of his right, it's the 'why' that interests my client.'

'I've got nothing more to say,' said Mrs. Maintree, and Adam Kane failed to get anything further out of her. She was either very clever or very innocent. She had offered no explanation for her relationship with Henderson and so there was nothing that could *be* checked. And she was perfectly within her rights to refuse, because there was nothing against her.

Mr. Kane returned to his office and

worked on some of the other matters that required his attention, but Thomas Henderson's will kept niggling away at the back of his mind and in the afternoon he went to interview the two witnesses concerned.

One was a jobbing gardener named Sidney Berts and the other was a Mrs. Sarah Martin, who helped with the cleaning, both of them being employed at the late Thomas Henderson's house, 'Northgates'.

They each told the same story. Mr. Benyon had asked them to come to the sickroom where Mr. Henderson lay in bed. They had been told that they were required to act as witnesses to his will. Thomas Henderson had been a very sick man but, although his breathing was laboured and he was exceedingly weak, seemed to know what he was doing. They had watched him sign his name feebly and with difficulty, and then, as directed by Mr. Benyon, they each signed theirs.

They had not been aware of the contents of the will — it was not legally necessary that they should — and the entire proceedings had occupied less than five minutes. And that was all. Not one single microscopic grain from which a case could be built for contesting the validity of the will. Everything had been done strictly in accordance with the correct legal practice.

When Mr. Kane got back to his office Anna Kesson was waiting with his letters to sign.

'That man, Sedgwick,' she said, while he was busy with his pen, 'witness in the McBride case, is unreliable. Five years ago he committed perjury, swearing he was only the nominee when, in fact, he was the principal.'

'Fine! We'll get a verdict for the defendant,' said Kane. As soon as he was alone, he lit a cigarette, and began to think. For over an hour he thought and chain-smoked and then he dialled a number. In the course of his professional career, Mr. Kane had acquired a number of unethical contacts as sources of information, and he started a number of sensitive antennae quivering as the result of his call.

Nothing more could be done until the

replies to his inquiries came in so he locked up the offices and left to take a certain interesting young lady out to dinner.

It was the middle of the afternoon on the following day when the reports from Adam Kane's unorthodox network kept the telephone busy. At a few minutes to five, he rang up Mr. Benyon.

'In the matter of the late Thomas Henderson's will,' said Kane, when Mr. Benyon came on the line, 'I am lodging a caveat at the Probate Court. Thought I'd let you know.' He rang off before Mr. Benyon could reply.

Less than twenty minutes elapsed before Mr. Benyon arrived.

'I was extremely surprised to hear that you intend to enter a caveat,' he said. 'I really cannot see on what grounds . . . '

'Sit down,' broke in Mr. Kane, 'and I'll tell you. The will is a fraud.'

'But that is quite impossible . . . '

'Just keep quiet and listen,' snapped Kane. 'During the last few years you've been getting yourself into a worse and worse financial mess. You tried speculating on the Stock Exchange and that went wrong. To bolster up your losses and save a crash, you used funds that had been entrusted to you by clients. At last you not only faced ruin but a charge of embezzlement. You tried everywhere to raise money and failed.

'And then Thomas Henderson sent for you and explained that he wanted to make his will. He'd put it off, as men do, until he realised how ill he was. He wanted to leave everything to his son — his son would have inherited, anyway, as next of kin but Henderson wanted to make sure . . . '

'This is absolute nonsense,' began Mr. Benyon, but Kane ignored the interruption.

'You saw how you could save yourself,' he went on. 'Henderson was dying. All you had to do was to substitute the name of 'Isobel Maintree' for 'Alec Henderson'. Nothing else altered at all. When you read the will to Thomas Henderson, of course, you read the name of his son as beneficiary. No doubt you had a copy of the will with you with Alec Henderson's name as beneficiary in case he wanted to read it for himself. It would have been easy to switch them. But he was too weak to bother. So the will making Isobel Maintree the beneficiary was duly attested, signed and witnessed, and the thing was done. Neat and almost foolproof.'

'It is entirely untrue,' said Benyon. 'You have no evidence to support such an outrageous suggestion . . .'

Mr. Kane grinned wickedly.

'An inquiry into your affairs would soon provide some. It would also turn up the fact that Mrs. Isobel Maintree's maiden name was Kitchen and that she is, in fact, your niece. It was a good scheme — so long as nobody suspected there was anything wrong. And why should they? Mrs. Maintree's attitude of refusing to discuss her 'relationship' with Henderson and offering no explanation why he should have made her his beneficiary — your instructions? — stopped any possibility of checking up. On the face of it you didn't benefit at all under the will. How was anyone to suspect that Mrs. Maintree was only your nominee? I'll bet you were going to let her have enough out of the swindle to bathe in gin for the rest of her life!'

★ ★ ★

'I never thought you'd pull it off,' said a jubilant Alec Henderson when he was told the news. 'It's marvellous! I can't tell you how grateful I feel.'

'Maybe you'll feel less grateful when you get my bill,' said Mr. Kane.

3

A Flush in Diamonds

Mr. Adam Kane's office hours were often as unconventional as the rest of his unorthodox legal practice. It was seldom that he saw a client unless a preliminary appointment had been made by his very efficient secretary, and so he was in the habit of arriving at his office at all hours, sometimes not until the afternoon if there was nothing important to attend to, for Mr. Kane often kept very late hours and always due to the exigencies of business.

He could rely on Anna Kesson to look after everything with her smooth, business-like assurance in his absence and to telephone him at his flat, very discreetly, if anything turned up that necessitated his immediate presence.

On this particular day his first appearance at the office was in the middle of the afternoon, and Anna Kesson drew her conclusions concerning the diversions of the previous night.

'Anything interesting?' asked Mr. Kane, before going through to his private office.

'Srimbal and Lacket have agreed to pay,' she said. 'There's a cheque in the post.'

Mr. Kane grinned sardonically.

'Damn fools! I was only bluffing. Couldn't've done a thing if they'd stuck out.'

He looked round quickly as the outer door opened hesitantly and a small, grey-haired wisp of a woman came in.

'Why, Mrs. Mears, what are you doing here in the afternoon?' asked Anna. 'Did you leave something behind this morning?'

'No, miss,' answered the little woman. 'I'm in great trouble. I come because I 'oped you might be able to 'elp me, sir, seein' you know all about the law . . . '

'What have you been up to, Mrs. Mears?' asked Mr. Kane.

'It's not me, sir,' said Mrs. Mears. 'It's my son, Charley. They've gone an' arrested 'im for stealin' a lady's jewels an' he didn't do it, sir: 'e don't know nothin' more about it than a babe unborn . . . '

'In that case, he's got nothing to worry about,' said Mr. Kane. 'Come in and tell me all about it.'

He led her into his private office, ensconced her in the shabby easy chair reserved for clients, and sat down behind his broad, scrupulously neat desk.

The little woman, almost swallowed up by the big chair, and nervously twisting a rag of a handkerchief in reddened hands, was responsible for cleaning the offices.

He remembered catching vague glimpses of her with brushes and pail on the rare occasions when he had been early.

'Now,' said Mr. Kane, lighting a cigarette, 'Let's have the whole story.'

'The whole story' with all Mrs. Mears' deviations removed, was a very simple one. Her son, Charley, who had just turned nineteen, worked for a firm of window cleaners in the West End, and one of his jobs was to clean the windows of Addinghall Court, a small but select block of flats in Knightsbridge.

There were only three flats, it had been

a conversion from a house, but these were large and spacious with every modern amenity. The middle flat was occupied by Sir Gordon Partridge and his wife and it was Lady Partridge's jewels — a diamond necklace, earrings, and a bracelet, that Charley Mears was supposed to have stolen.

'But 'e didn't know nothin' about 'em,' said Mrs. Mears, getting tearful and using the screwed-up handkerchief ineffectually. 'Not even that they was there, 'e didn't.'

'When was he arrested?' asked Mr. Kane.

'Last night they come for 'im. Eatin' 'is supper, he was, when they come . . . '

Mrs. Mears paused to sniff and dab at her eyes.

'Searched the 'ole 'ouse, they did, but they didn't find nothin'. 'Ow could they? There wasn't nothin' to find.'

'Why didn't you tell my secretary about this earlier this morning?'

'I didn't do the offices this mornin' sir,' said Mrs. Mears. 'I was that upset . . . '

Mr. Kane picked up the telephone receiver. In a few seconds he was speaking to the sergeant in charge of the police station where Charley Mears would have been taken.

'You've got a man named Mears, charged with stealing jewellery from a flat in . . . Adam Kane speaking . . . Divisional-Inspector Ogden . . . ? Yes, put him on.'

Mr. Kane stubbed out his cigarette in the big cut-glass ashtray.

'Ogden? This is Kane . . . Not too bad. How're you? Listen, about this chap, Mears . . . '

The telephone vibrated to the deep rumble of Ogden's voice as it broke into Kane's question. Kane listened until it paused

'Well, when *do* you intend to charge him?' he asked. 'You can't keep him 'helping with your inquiries' long. You'll have to charge him or let him go . . . Yes, I'm acting for him. I shall be along to see him in about an hour . . . Yes, I'd like a word with you, too.'

Mr. Kane put the phone back on its rack and lit another cigarette.

'Your son hasn't actually been charged

yet,' he said. 'But he soon will be. I'm going to see him.'

'Can you 'elp 'im, sir?' asked Mrs. Mears, eagerly.

'I don't know what I can do, until I know the whole of the facts,' said Mr. Kane. 'Go into my secretary's office and she'll give you a cup of tea. Then go home. You'll hear from me, later.'

★　★　★

Charley Mears was a thin youth, taller than his mother, with a mop of long brown hair and sullen eyes, masking his inward fear by an outward show of truculent bravado.

''Ave you come to get me out of 'ere?' he asked, when Adam Kane told him who he was. 'The bloody fuzz ain't got no right to keep me 'ere . . . '

'Keep that chip off your shoulder,' snapped Mr. Kane, 'if you expect me to help you. Did you steal those diamonds?'

'No. Didn't know there *was* any bloody diamonds until the fuzz told me. 'Ow should I?'

198

Mr. Kane lit a cigarette and gave one to Mears who took it eagerly, but without thanks.

'When do you clean these windows at Addinghall Court?' he asked. 'How often?'

'Every three weeks.'

'Yesterday was the usual date, was it? What time?'

'It 'ud be about 'alf past twelve, I s'pose.'

'Was there anyone in the flat — the Partridges' flat, I mean, when you cleaned the windows?'

'They was both there when I started, but they went out — when I'd 'alf finished. Saw 'em drive off in their car.'

'Do you go inside the flats to clean the windows?'

'No. I only do the outside.'

'But you could get inside through one of the windows easily?'

'I could, but I didn't.'

'Who occupies the other two flats?'

'Bloke called Lumley an' 'is wife live in the top one. Beavers, who 'as the bottom flat, used ter 'ave the Partridges but they swopped over about six months back.'

'What order do you clean the flats?'

'Start at the top an' work down.'

'So you cleaned the windows of the bottom flat last. What did you do then?'

'Went on ter me next job. What's the good of all these bloody questions? Just get me out of 'ere . . . '

'I'm going to get you charged,' said Mr. Kane.

Mears stared, open-mouthed.

'What the 'ell d'yer mean?' he demanded. 'I thought you was goin' to 'elp me . . . '

'That's what I'm doing,' answered Adam Kane.

* * *

He found Divisional-Detective-Inspector Ogden in his office, waiting for him, squeezed into a chair behind his desk and smoking a large pipe.

'How did you get on with Mears?' he inquired.

'When are you charging him?' said Mr. Kane, curtly. 'You've either got to charge him or let him go.'

'We're charging him,' said Ogden. 'I was waiting in the hope that he'd be sensible an' tell us what he'd done with the stuff.'

'Couldn't if he'd never had it, could he?' said Mr. Kane. 'What's the value of the stolen property?'

'Accordin' to Lady Partridge, eight thousand pounds.'

Mr. Kane pursed up his lips in a silent whistle.

'And you haven't found it? H'm. Mears'll be up before the magistrates in the morning, will he?'

Ogden removed his pipe from his heavy face and nodded.

'I shall ask for a remand,' said Mr. Kane.

'We shall oppose bail . . . '

'Shan't ask for it,' broke in Mr. Kane. 'See you tomorrow.'

It was half-past five when Adam Kane left Ogden and drove to Addinghall Court via a small shop in Soho that sold pornographic literature, lurid-jacketed novels, and tobacco, among other things. It was one of his more respectable sources of information.

The stout, bald-headed man, whose button eyes twinkled at Kane through steel-rimmed spectacles, listened to his request in an untidy room behind the shop that smelt of old paper, newsprint and drains.

'You want the low-down on these three people, Mr. Kane,' he said, scribbling the names down on a piece of old newspaper. 'I can tell you about Lewis Beavers now. He runs a string of hot-spots and clip-joints. Must be making a packet. Got in bad with the protection racket boys a few months ago . . . '

'Let me have all the details you can get hold of,' Mr. Kane cut him short. 'About this whole crowd — and put some guts into it. I want the information this evening. You can phone me at my office.'

Sir Gordon Partridge and his wife were not overjoyed when Adam Kane presented himself at the flat and explained why he was there.

'You'll have to make it snappy,' said Sir Gordon, who was a man of about forty-five with pale yellow hair and a reddish face. 'We're going out and we

202

haven't started to dress yet.'

'What I want won't take very long,' said Mr. Kane.

'We told the police all we knew,' put in Lady Partridge. 'There's not much more we can tell you.'

Mr. Kane's looked at the woman who was leaning back in a corner of the huge leather-covered settee and decided that she was well worth looking at. She was much younger than her husband with long, dark hair that had a sheen where it caught the light, like the smooth surface of sealskin, and her eyes were large and of a greenish-amber. He would have to concentrate very hard, he thought, to keep from looking at her legs which were exquisite and very well displayed.

'Why were you so certain that it was the window cleaner, Mears, who took your diamonds?' he asked.

'It couldn't have been anybody else,' said Sir Gordon. 'We were only out a couple of hours and they'd gone when we got back. There was no sign of a break-in . . . '

'Nobody else got a key?'

Sir Gordon shook his head.

'You haven't lost or mislaid your own keys recently?'

'No.'

'You're quite sure the diamonds were still here when you went out?'

'Yes.' It was Lady Partridge who answered this time. 'I went to my jewel-case to get a gold pin to fasten my scarf . . . '

'The jewel-case was taken as well, wasn't it?'

'The whole blasted lot,' said her husband. 'Unless they're found it's a dead loss . . . '

'You can claim the insurance . . . '

'Can we hell! The damn things weren't insured.'

'How was that?' asked Mr. Kane.

'Well, it was really my wife's fault,' began Sir Gordon. 'You see . . . '

'I thought Gordon had insured them,' interposed his wife.

'What you really mean is that you forgot,' said her husband. 'I only found out that they hadn't been insured when we took 'em out of the bank at the beginning of the week. My wife wanted to wear 'em at a 'do' we went to. As soon as

I knew the things weren't insured I decided to get it done at once. Now it's blasted well too late!'

'Did you give them to your wife?' asked Mr. Kane.

'They originally belonged to my aunt,' explained Sir Gordon. 'When she died she left 'em to me . . . '

'And you gave them to your wife. I see.' Mr. Kane got up. 'Well, I hope you get them back. Eight thousand pounds is quite a lot to lose.'

★　★　★

When Mr. Kane got back to his office Anna Kesson had gone but she had left several letters on his desk for him to sign. He scribbled his signature on them, lit a cigarette, and settled himself comfortably in the padded chair behind his desk to think.

At half-past eight the telephone bell rang and he grabbed the receiver from its rack, pulled a notepad nearer and picked up a pencil. In his ear cackled the rather shrill voice of the Soho shopkeeper.

Mr. Kane listened attentively, jotting down a few notes on the pad beside him, interpolating a brief question now and again. For nearly half an hour the crackling voice went on and at the end of that period, Mr. Kane had acquired a considerable amount of information concerning the inhabitants of Addinghall Court.

He considered all the various facts he had learned and at the expiration of three cigarettes had reached two possible solutions. The difficulty was to prove which was right, if either of them were. And there was the time factor which didn't help.

There was one way but it was drastic and the repercussion, if it went wrong, could be serious. But he only hesitated for a few seconds. His entire practice had been built on hunches and risks, though perhaps it was more a kind of unusual ability to assess the essentials quicker than other people.

Mr. Kane looked up the address of one of his more disreputable acquaintances and left the office.

In the softly lit, very select and expensive restaurant, Mr. Kane offered his companion a cigarette, lit it for her, took one himself, and inhaled deeply. The girl who sat beside him on the padded couch, a pretty red-head, prattled on happily, but Mr. Kane, although he seemed to be listening, heard very little of what she said. It was nearly a quarter to twelve and he was waiting for the result of the plan he had set in operation earlier that evening.

At twelve o'clock, a little, thin man, with small beady eyes set very close to the jutting bridge of his large nose, was conducted to Mr. Kane's table by a waiter.

'All right?' asked Mr. Kane.

'Okay,' said the little man, and held up his thumbs.

Mr. Kane rose to his feet.

'Time to go home, darling,' he said to the girl, and signed the bill which the waiter had already laid on the table.

★　★　★

The morning papers were being pushed through the letter boxes when Mr. Kane, a parcel under one arm, rang the bell of the middle flat at Addinghall Court.

He had to ring several times before the door was opened by Sir Gordon Partridge, clad in a silk dressing gown, and still half asleep.

'Good God, what the hell do you want at this hour?' he demanded.

'Let me come in and I'll tell you,' said Mr. Kane. Without waiting he pushed past Sir Gordon and entered the lounge. 'I've brought back your diamonds.'

He tore the paper off the parcel.

'Your wife's jewel-case,' he said.

'But this is marvellous,' exclaimed Partridge. 'How did you find it? Wait a minute, I must tell my wife. She'll be delighted . . . '

After a very short interval Lady Partridge came in.

She looked attractive; bewildered, but anything but delighted.

'There's your jewel-case,' said Mr. Kane, curtly. 'You needn't bother to get the diamonds insured. They're not worth it.'

'What do you mean?' demanded Sir Gordon.

'Ask your wife,' snapped Mr. Kane. 'She had them copied so that she could sell the real ones. When you decided to get them insured she naturally panicked. The insurance company would have them valued before issuing a policy and the whole thing would blow up. So she stole her own jewel-case . . . '

'Is this true?' Sir Gordon turned to his wife and saw the answer in her face.

'I'll tell you where the jewel-case was found,' went on Mr. Kane, remorselessly. 'In this flat, hidden in a locked drawer of your wife's dressing table.' Mr. Kane could look very virtuous when it suited him and the expression on his dark face as he looked at Lady Partridge was contemptuous. 'You didn't care what might happen to Mears. He was only a window cleaner. If he'd gone to prison for something he didn't do it wouldn't have caused you any lack of sleep. But he's my client and I'm going to advise him to issue a writ against you for libel . . . '

'You can't do that,' she exclaimed.

Mr. Kane grinned without mirth.

'Can't I? This is going to cost you a hell of a packet in damages . . . '

'How can it be libel . . . ?' she began, but her husband stopped her.

'You go back to bed,' he said curtly. 'I want to talk to Mr. Kane.'

★ ★ ★

'So, eventually, he agreed that it would be better to settle the matter without going to court,' said Mr. Kane, later that morning, explaining to his secretary. 'You can pay that into the bank when you go to lunch.'

He flipped a cheque on to her desk and she raised her eyebrows when she saw the amount.

'Two thousand pounds is a lot of money,' she said.

'Could've cost him a lot more and some nasty publicity. Laying false information, knowing it to be false, resulting in damaging the reputation of another person is a serious offence.' Mr. Kane lit a cigarette. 'Charley Mears ought to be home by now. The charge has been dropped.'

'How did you work it all out?' asked Anna Kesson.

'If Mears hadn't pinched the diamonds it looked like an inside job. Lewis Beavers seemed the best bet. He'd swopped flats with the Partridges and could've hung on to a key, and his reputation was pretty stinking. Then I learned that Lady Partridge had been badly in debt six months ago, threatened with writs all over the place. And then suddenly she paid up. When they told me about the insurance I guessed what might have happened. It was a toss-up between Lady Partridge and Beavers. There was one way to find out, have both the flats searched while the tenants were out. So, I engaged an expert to do just that. Luckily he started with the Partridges' flat and got the jackpot.'

'You'll take a risk too many one of these days,' said Miss Kesson, disapprovingly.

Mr. Kane grinned.

'Maybe,' he said. 'By the way, one thousand five hundred of that cheque goes to the Mearses. You'd better advise 'em the best thing to do with it.'

'What happens to the other five hundred?'

'My fee and costs,' answered Mr. Kane. 'Expert burglars are expensive!'

4

Ransom for a Wife

Adam Kane first met Leon Marsholt when the latter kept a small general shop in an outer suburb of London. Kane, at that time, was holding down a job as clerk in a solicitor's office, in the same district. He bought most of his supplies from the little corner shop which sold practically everything.

By the time that Kane had set up in his own legal practice, Marsholt had acquired four shops, and four years later, was chairman and managing director of a company owning a chain of supermarkets extending from the south to the north of England, and well on the way to becoming a millionaire.

Adam Kane had been responsible for handling all Marsholt's legal business for over ten years. It was one of the few orthodox jobs in his very unorthodox

213

practice, for Adam Kane specialised in more unusual problems than the ordinary lawyer and, in consequence, had acquired rather a peculiar reputation.

When Marsholt met and subsequently married Linda Kerr, a young and very attractive television small-part actress, Kane had had certain misgivings. She was in her early twenties, and he was already past his middle fifties, rather stodgy in his outlook and set in his ways. Although Kane was pretty certain that Marsholt was in love with his wife, he wasn't nearly so sure that she was in love with her husband. There was very little to charm a woman in Marsholt. He was stolid, dull, and except in his own business, not particularly intelligent. Kane, whose long contact with various forms of human nature had made him cynical, had concluded that Marsholt's attraction for the lovely Linda lay in his bank.

But, apparently, he was wrong, for after two and a half years of marriage they seemed to be extremely happy. Marsholt looked younger, had put on weight, and radiated happiness and content.

Adam Kane hadn't seen him for over a fortnight when without any previous appointment Marsholt burst into his office, ignoring the protests of Kane's secretary.

'Kane, you've got to help me. I'm almost out of mind . . . '

Kane thought he looked it. The roundness of his face had become flabby and his eyes had sunk among a sea of wrinkles, the red-rimmed lids suggesting lack of sleep.

'Good God, Marsholt,' exclaimed Kane, 'what the hell's the matter?'

Marsholt dropped heavily into the clients' chair. With shaking hands he fumbled in his pocket.

'It's Linda,' he said, and his voice sounded as if all the moisture in his throat had dried up. 'It's Linda — she's been kidnapped!'

'Kidnapped?' Kane had expected something quite different — his previous fears realised at last. 'When?'

'Four days ago.' Marsholt's uncertain fingers found the packet of cigarettes he was searching for. 'They phoned and said they'd got her . . . ' He managed to take out a cigarette but dropped it. 'It's been hell . . . I can't sleep — I've scarcely eaten . . . '

'Why didn't you tell me before?' Kane got up quickly, came round the broad desk, gave Marsholt the cigarette and lit it for him. 'You'd better tell me now — everything.'

Marsholt drew in the smoke with a long, rasping intake and started coughing violently. Kane went over to a cabinet, took out a bottle of whisky, splashed some into a glass and brought it to Marsholt.

'Drink this,' he said. 'It'll steady you up. Don't spill it, man!'

Marsholt's hand was shaking so badly that the whisky almost slopped over the side of the glass. He managed to sip a little and then a little more.

'What can I do?' he said, and his voice was less of a croak. 'There must be something I can do . . . '

'Until I know exactly what's happened, I can't tell you,' said Kane, going back to the chair behind the desk. 'Let's have the whole story from the beginning.'

'There isn't much I can tell you.' Marsholt swallowed the rest of the whisky and nursed the empty glass in his lap. 'I don't know — that's what's driving me round the bend. This silence . . . '

'You mean you've heard nothing since you got the phone call? What did it say?'

'That they'd got Linda. If I wanted to see her again I was to do nothing until they got in touch with me again. If I told the police, or anyone, she'd be killed. But I've heard nothing, I tell you, nothing . . . ' Marsholt drew on his cigarette but it had gone out. 'I've sat by the phone — all the time. I haven't left the flat. I cancelled everything — said I was ill . . . ' His voice rose up the scale. 'I'd do anything — pay anything — to get Linda back.'

'You'll hear,' said Kane. 'They're letting you sweat. The more you sweat, the easier it'll be to get what they want. That's how the racket works. How did they manage to get hold of your wife?'

'She'd gone to see a friend — a girl she knew when she was in TV. We were going out — I've had to be away a lot, lately, and hadn't had time to see much of her . . . Linda never came back to the flat . . . She was going to get back at six . . . I phoned Eileen, the girl, her friend, but she hadn't been there. The phone call came through just as I put down the receiver . . .'

Marsholt got up abruptly. The empty glass fell on the floor and rolled under Kane's desk. 'I shouldn't have come here,' he exclaimed. 'I should have stayed the night. They may have phoned . . .'

'If they have, they'll phone again,' broke in Kane. 'Go back, have a good meal, and relax. As soon as they contact you, phone me. Don't *do* anything. You needn't worry that Linda will be harmed, she won't. You don't destroy the goods you hope to sell.'

When Marsholt had gone, Mr. Kane smoked three cigarettes, staring up through the bluish-white trails of vaporised tobacco but seeing nothing of the discoloured ceiling. Then he unlocked a drawer, took out a small, shabby notebook and riffled the pages. In the course of his professional career, Mr. Kane had acquired sources of possible information that his brethren of the law would have regarded as unethical.

On his private phone that had a direct

outside line, he made three calls of varying duration, hoping that the sensitive nerves he had set quivering would react with the right response. Over the intercom, he asked his efficient secretary to look up the address of Miss Eileen Beresford in the Telephone Directory.

'I'm going out, Anna,' he said, when she brought it to him. 'If Mr. Marsholt rings up, give him Miss Beresford's number and tell him to ring me there.'

* * *

Adam Kane pressed the bell of the third floor flat in Conway Mansions, Hampstead, and hoped that Eileen Beresford would be in. She was, and when he explained briefly who he was, she took him into a comfortable, but very untidy, sitting room.

She was a dark woman of about thirty-two who just missed being pretty.

She listened to what Kane told her in a kind of doubtful surprise.

'Kidnapped Linda?' she said. 'How awful. Poor old Leon. He must be doing his nut! Of course, I didn't worry when she didn't turn up . . . '

'Why 'of course'?' interjected Kane.

'Linda's like that,' she answered. 'She'll make a date with you but you can never be sure she'll keep it. If something more exciting cropped up — well, that was that.'

'Without a word, eh?'

'Oh yes, it didn't occur to her, you see. She'd be full of excuses and apologies the next time she saw you. That's why I didn't bother when she didn't come. I just thought she'd run into one of her club friends and changed her mind . . . '

'Club friends?' said Kane quickly.

With a childish gesture she covered her mouth with the back of her hand.

'I didn't mean to say that,' she said. 'Don't tell Leon, will you? He was away a lot and she got bored . . . '

'Tell me which clubs.'

'The *Afgar*, the *Golden Spinner* . . . '

'She didn't go alone,' said Kane. 'Who took her?'

'Harry Gherril — he's a TV producer . . . ' She looked at him with troubled eyes. 'Don't tell Leon, please . . . '

'I'll think about it,' said Adam Kane.

He had scarcely got back to his office when the telephone buzzed insistently. It was the direct line phone and he listened while it chattered in his ear, scrawling a few notes on the pad beside him. One of the 'nerves' had reacted better than he had hoped. A few minutes later Marsholt rang.

'I've heard from them,' he said. 'They want twenty thousand pounds.'

'It's a lot of money,' began Kane. 'Are you . . . '

'If it was twice that, I'd pay it,' interrupted Marsholt. 'I'm going to the bank, now, to get it . . . '

'Listen,' said Kane, and changed his mind. 'I'm coming to see you. Don't do anything more until I get there.' He rang off before Marsholt had time to reply and left the office. On his way to Marsholt's flat he thought over what he knew and tried to decide on the best way to handle it. Marsholt respected money. He was careful with the spending of it, mean in some ways. That he made no demur at paying twenty thousand pounds to get his wife back showed just how much he must love her. Mr. Kane wondered if Linda appreciated that . . .

Marsholt opened the door of the flat himself and followed Kane into the lounge.

'There's nothing you can do,' he said. 'I can manage this myself, now. It was the silence — not hearing anything — not knowing — that got me down . . . '

'How are you going to deliver the money?' asked Kane.

'I promised I wouldn't tell anyone,' answered Marsholt. 'Gave my word. Linda will be back this evening. They'll bring her near here and let her go. That's the arrangement . . . '

'How do you know they'll keep it?' said Kane.

'Why shouldn't they? They'll have got the money.'

'You're not going to tell me how?' said Kane.

Marsholt shook his head.

'No. I'll keep my part of the bargain,' he said.

★ ★ ★

Adam Kane eased the pressure of his foot on the accelerator as Marsholt's car ahead began to lose speed. There was a side turning a little further on and he swung into it and stopped. Hurriedly he got out and ran back.

Marsholt's car was stationary at the side of the road, and Kane let his lungs deflate in relief. After following him so far he didn't want to lose him at the last moment. Marsholt got out of his car and Kane saw that he was carrying a suitcase. The money, obviously. The street was ugly and drab, dirty walls of brick with large wooden gates at irregular intervals. Just beyond where Marsholt had stopped his car was a telephone box, set out a foot from the wall.

Marsholt looked up and down the street but Kane was hidden by the wall of the turning. He watched Marsholt move towards the telephone box. A clock, somewhere, struck six, and Marsholt came back to his car, no longer carrying the suitcase. After a quick glance all round, he got back in the car and drove away.

Adam Kane was not interested in

Marsholt any more. He wanted to see who came to pick up the suitcase which Marsholt had left between the back of the telephone box and the wall . . . In less than five minutes his curiosity was satisfied. Someone appeared at the other end of the street and walked quickly along to the telephone box. The suitcase was picked out from its resting place and then the person who had received it turned — and faced Mr. Kane!

'My car's just round the corner,' he remarked, pleasantly. '*I'll* take the suit-case . . . '

★ ★ ★

'What are you going to do?' asked Linda Marsholt, glancing sideways at Mr. Kane behind the wheel of his car.

'I'm taking you back to your husband, you and the money,' he answered, without looking at her.

'He'll never forgive me,' she said a little uneasily. '*Must* you tell him — the truth? He'd be happier not — not to know . . . '

'Do you expect me to compound a

felony?' said Kane.

'It wasn't a felony . . . '

'Call it what you like, it was a cruel and heartless thing to do.'

'You don't understand — you don't understand at all!' she burst out passionately. 'I was at my wits' end — I didn't know what to do. I had to find that money . . . '

Adam Kane slowed down and slid efficiently into a parking place between a line of other cars.

'Now, listen,' he said. 'I know the whole story. 'I got bored when my husband was so often away.' Like a bloody fool you started gambling, it was a thrill. As Marsholt's wife you were welcomed at those two clubs, the *Afgar* and the *Golden Spinner*. They're always on the lookout for mugs and they let you have all the credit you wanted — on Marsholt's name . . . '

'I — I didn't know I owed so much. When they told me it was nearly twenty thousand pounds I couldn't believe it . . . '

'They threatened to go to your husband, didn't they? So you thought up this precious little scheme — at least you

225

didn't *think* anything up. You pinched the whole idea. There was nothing remotely original in it. You didn't care what it might do to Marsholt.'

'I was frightened — terrified what he might do, if he found out. He hates gambling . . . '

'And that's *all* you thought about, *yourself*,' said Kane. 'Didn't you think that the shock, worry and anxiety could have had a really serious effect on Marsholt? Don't you realise how very deeply he loves you?'

She was crying, gently, almost unconsciously, the tears running down her face and dropping on her lap.

'I love Leon, too,' she said. 'You don't believe I do, but I do. I — I knew how he would feel . . . having to *pay* all that money. He always makes a fuss if he has to pay out large amounts of money . . . '

'He didn't make any fuss about this,' said Kane. 'In fact, he was willing to pay twice the amount to have you back . . . Who did you get to help you? Who did the phoning to Marsholt? Cherril?'

'No, it was an actor I know . . . I'm not telling you his name. I don't want to involve anyone else . . . ' She paused. 'Let's go,' she said. 'Leon is expecting me at the flat. That was the arrangement. As soon as he'd delivered the money I was to be released near the flat . . . '

'We'll give him a double reason for celebrating,' said Adam Kane. 'We'll bring him you and the money. Don't worry. I'm not going to give you away. But don't be a fool again. We'll let Marsholt believe that it was all true . . . '

'But when he hears about the money I owe . . . ' she began.

'Leave it to me,' said Kane. 'He won't know anything about that. I know quite a lot about the man who runs both those clubs. He's crooked and the games are crooked. You won't hear any more.'

THE END

We do hope that you have enjoyed reading this large print book.

Did you know that all of our titles are available for purchase?

We publish a wide range of high quality large print books including:
Romances, Mysteries, Classics
General Fiction
Non Fiction and Westerns

Special interest titles available in large print are:
The Little Oxford Dictionary
Music Book, Song Book
Hymn Book, Service Book

Also available from us courtesy of Oxford University Press:
Young Readers' Dictionary
(large print edition)
Young Readers' Thesaurus
(large print edition)

For further information or a free brochure, please contact us at:
Ulverscroft Large Print Books Ltd.,
The Green, Bradgate Road, Anstey,
Leicester, LE7 7FU, England.
Tel: (00 44) **0116 236 4325**
Fax: (00 44) **0116 234 0205**

Other titles in the
Linford Mystery Library:

THE DARK CORNERS
& OTHER STORIES

Robert J. Tilley

A schoolboy disappears — but the missing child may not be all he seemed . . . A mortician and his family find their new neighbours disturbingly interested in their affairs . . . Quiet Mr. Wooller finds himself the only man ready to take down the Devil . . . An escaped convict stumbles upon an apparently idyllic holiday cottage . . . A spouses' golf game ends in murder . . . In an outwardly perfect marriage, one partner is making dark dealings . . . A young man is subjected to a bizarre hostage-taking . . . Seven unsettling stories from the pen of Robert J. Tilley.

THE SYMBOL SEEKERS

A. A. Glynn

In 1867 a box treasured by a distinguished American exile in England is stolen. Three battle-hardened ex-Southern soldiers from the recently ended American Civil War arrive on an unusual mission: two go on a hectic pursuit of the box in Liverpool and London, whilst third takes a path that could lead to the gallows. Detective Septimus Dacers and Roberta Van Trask, the daughter of an American diplomat, risk their lives as they attempt to foil a grotesque scheme that could cause war between Britain and the United States . . .

SONS OF THE SPHINX

Norman Firth

'We have read of your intended expedition to Egypt, to the Pyramid of Khufu . . . Only death can be your lot if you embark upon this journey. The Sons of the Sphinx.' So reads the sinister message in fine Arabic script mailed to a Hollywood movie producer. But the filming goes ahead — and the body of his chief cameraman is found with his throat cut . . . While in *Corpses Don't Care*, the grand opening of a luxury hotel is ruined by a series of six corpses turning up in the most inconvenient places!

THE LION'S GATE

V. J. Banis

On holiday with her wayward sister Allison at a lakeside town, Peggy Conners is perplexed when Allison packs her bags and vanishes overnight, without explanation. Believing her sister to be in great danger, Peggy eventually traces and confronts her, now living on an island at the Lions family mansion. But then Allison asserts that her name is actually Melissa Lions — and that she has never seen Peggy before in her life!